"Carefully detailed . . . Although Melville's plot is perfectly satisfying, the style of the author's writing remains his strong suit. . . . Melville's measured pace has a feeling of being precisely tailored to the exotic locale that he seems to know so well."

Philadelphia Inquirer

"A cleverly hatched plot and the Japanese environment is authentic. Demure Hanae turns out to be quite a detective herself who has more than one netsuke up her sleeve."

Chattanooga Times

"This engrossing tale is much more than a model of what a police procedural story should be. Mr. Melville understands the national character of the Japanese. . . . a good story."

Manchester, New Hampshire, Union Leader

"An ingenious page-turner . . . artful suspense."

Booklist

"Mystery fans and art lovers alike will enjoy this new case in the career of Japan's Superintendent Otani. . . . The charm of the Japanese setting and the intriguing characters make this delightful reading."

Saqinaw, Michigan, News

Fawcett Crest Books
by James Melville:

THE WAGES OF ZEN

A SORT OF SAMURAI

THE CHRYSANTHEMUM CHAIN

THE NINTH NETSUKE

James Melville

FAWCETT CREST • NEW YORK

A Fawcett Crest Book
Published by Ballantine Books
Copyright © 1982 by James Melville

First published in England 1982

ISBN 0-449-20823-0

This edition published by arrangement with St. Martin's Press

Manufactured in the United States of America

First Ballantine Books Edition: August 1986

For John Blackwell, who makes them better

AUTHOR'S NOTE

Hyogo is a real prefecture, and it has a police force.
It should be emphasised therefore that all the characters in this story are wholly fictitious and bear no
relation to any actual person, living or dead.

最後の根付け

Chapter I

"**W**ELL," SAID TETSUO OTANI TO HIS WIFE HANAE, "surely you wouldn't prefer me to come with somebody else?" Hanae gave him a wary sidelong glance.

It was a beautiful afternoon in late autumn, and they were making their way up a narrow hilly street just north of the main Motomachi shopping area in Kobe. Superintendent Otani's face was set in its habitual expressionless gravity, but he met Hanae's glance from the corner of his eye and she found herself unable to sustain the prim manner she had adopted when they left the station and she finally accepted that her husband seriously intended to go through with the project.

"The very idea," she huffed in pretended outrage. "It's just that it seems so ridiculous, at our age. They're bound to suspect." Otani stopped outside the little open-fronted grocery shop they were passing and looked Hanae up and down. She was in her forties, but could have fibbed five years off her age without the least trouble. Possibly out of sheer embarrassment, she had taken longer than usual over

1

her make-up, and was wearing a soft blue silk dress which Otani had bought her with some of his summer bonus.

He lifted a finger and wagged it at her. "Ha-chan, you look very attractive and very embarrassed. The perfect picture of a guilty married lady off for a quiet afternoon with her distinguished-looking lover."

Hanae sighed and shook her head with resignation. "It seems such an extraordinary thing to do. There really are a lot of these places, are there?"

Otani looked around, then pointed. "Look, see the one with the turrets like a castle? That's the Hawaii. Just behind it is the Blue Grotto. The Imperial and the Fantasia are around the corner. At least fifty of them in Kobe alone, all with between a dozen and twenty rooms, and most of those let three or four times a day at a minimum. Take it from me, there are a lot of respectable middle-aged people enjoying themselves at this very moment."

They walked on, past restaurants with plastic spaghetti and sandwiches displayed in the windows, and rounded the corner. The Fantasia Hotel was no more than fifty metres along. Hanae's cheeks grew even pinker as they approached it past a garage which contained three cars. Each one had a placard bearing the name of the hotel in phonetic Japanese script propped carefully against the front fender to conceal the number-plate from the casual onlooker. She stopped short when she saw a large illuminated mauve glass sign with black lettering.

FANTASIA HOTEL
Automatic Round Beds
Colour Television
VTR
Mood Films
WELCOME. . . .Select the
Room of your Dreams
Short rest (2 hours)
from Y5,200
Night's Lodging
from Y8,500

"Darling, I *can't*," she faltered, but Otani was already half-way through the automatic glass-door, and somehow she managed to bring herself to enter.

There was another sign inside, with a series of colour photographs of the interiors of rooms. One was all chromium, glass and white carpets like a film star's boudoir; another was done up in vaguely Napoleonic style with a four-poster and Regency striped walls, while a third featured what might have been a water-bed and was hung with batik draperies. Other rooms were described only by name, and after a cursory glance at the list Otani crossed the tiny lobby to a glass window like a cinema ticket box. The glass at the top was obscured, and only a pair of female hands was visible.

"Is the Sweet Harmony Room available?" Otani demanded firmly, and almost at once a key was pushed through the aperture.

"You are welcome. Room 403, fourth floor," said a disembodied voice with a strong but not unpleasing Osaka accent, and Otani smiled briefly at Hanae as they entered the small lift. "See?" he said encouragingly. "They do their best not to make you feel embarrassed."

Hanae glanced down at the key with its pink plastic tag. "What would you have done if it had been occupied?" she asked. The lift stopped at their floor and Otani led the way to Room 403. A red light was blinking above the door. There were four other rooms in the short corridor. Two had red lights shining steadily, while the other two were not illuminated.

"I don't know," he replied as he opened the door. "I just hoped they wouldn't be too busy at this time of the day, and we were lucky." Hanae followed him into the room and blinked as she took it in. The principal feature of the décor was a large circular bed with mirrors on three sides, mounted on a kind of dais covered with artificial fur. In the corner beyond the bed was a television set with a camera to one side. A curtain, drawn back, separated the

3

bed area from the rest of the room, which contained a small wardrobe cupboard and a distinctly workaday occasional table and easy chair; a small refrigerator with a price list on top, and a shallow plastic simulated lacquer box containing two neatly folded cotton kimonos.

Hanae was still looking around her in wonderment, and gave a small shriek of amusement when she turned and examined the bathroom behind her. It was tiled in lurid emerald and gold, and beside a deep sunken bath there was an inflated air mattress. Her embarrassment forgotten, she wandered round the room, then slipped her shoes off and clambered on to the bed. Otani went and sat beside her, and after examining a console of buttons, pressed one. The bed began to rotate, making Hanae almost lose her balance. Otani made the bed stop by pressing another, while a third set it moving in the opposite direction. An infinity of Hanaes presented themselves as the mirrors came into alignment, and Otani stopped the motor again and pointed to them. "My idea of paradise," he commented. "Making love to lots of you at the same time."

Hanae blushed again, then looked at him seriously. "I suppose we ought to be ashamed of ourselves," she said quietly. "Behaving like silly children when that poor woman was killed in this very room. You're sure it *was* this room?"

Otani nodded. "Yes. Four nights ago. There's no doubt about it. I saw Kimura's report, and both the name and the number of the room are right." He lay back on the bed with his arms behind his head and stared at his reflection in the mirrored ceiling. "During the day these places really are mostly used by quite ordinary youngsters who have nowhere else to go to be alone. And business people. Lots of office affairs go on, you know. It's not till the evening that the bar girls and prostitutes bring their clients. I'm afraid this room has seen nasty as well as nice moments, Ha-chan. But commerce goes on, and the Fantasia Hotel was back in business within thirty-six hours after they found her body."

"Why did you want to come here yourself?" Hanae propped herself up on one elbow and looked down at Otani's face.

He reached out and pressed another switch before replying, but apparently nothing happened.

"It's Kimura's case, of course," he said ruminatively. "You never know with foreigners, though. I might easily find myself involved with some Consul or other . . . and things are rather quiet at the moment."

Hanae smiled. "You're bored, and you're going to get into poor Kimura-san's way again," she said.

Otani pulled a face at her. "I have no intention of doing any such thing," he said in a magisterial way. "Would you care for me to repeat that?" As Hanae looked at him blankly he rolled over and again played with the switches on the console at his side. "Watch," he commanded, and pointed at the television screen. It flickered into life and Hanae saw herself propped up on one elbow, looking down at her husband's face. Her mouth opened and closed, and Otani pulled a face. Then the screen went blank as he switched the contraption off.

"What on earth . . . ?"

"Videotape recorder. Part of the service," said Otani calmly. "I'd forgotten about no sound, though." Hanae began to clamber off the bed as though she had been stung, and Otani smiled. "Don't worry," he said reassuringly. "I'll erase the tape before we go."

"I don't think I like this place," said Hanae uncertainly. "May we leave now, please?"

"In a moment. I'll just have a bit of a look round," Otani replied, crossing to the refrigerator and opening it. Inside were cans of beer and Coca-Cola, packets of nuts and rice crackers, and a small bottle of Suntory whisky. "Care for a drink?" he enquired affably, but Hanae shook her head. Otani sat down in the easy chair beside the occasional table and popped open a can of Sapporo beer; hesitated, then decided to drink it straight from the can.

Hanae still lay on the bed, looking around the room in disbelief. "What did you expect to gain by coming here?" she asked, and Otani took another long pull from the can before replying.

"It's hard to say, really," he admitted. "Needless to say, the people who run this place began by claiming that they'd never seen the woman before in their lives, but as soon as Kimura started questioning the cleaning women it came out that she came here two or three nights a week, and almost always used this room."

"How would the cleaning women know?" Hanae was puzzled. "When we came in there didn't seem to be a soul about."

"You'll see when we leave," Otani said. "When people are ready to go they ring down to the desk and let them know what they've used from the refrigerator. Then somebody brings the bill up, and while the customer is paying the maid takes a quick look round the room to make sure it's in reasonable order. They have to be careful, otherwise people might wreck the place or slip out without paying. As soon as the door of the room is opened some sort of indicator flashes downstairs."

"You seem to know a lot about it," sniffed Hanae suspiciously, and Otani grinned at her, then finished off his beer.

"I know a lot about all sorts of things," he said calmly. "And what I don't know I ask Ninja or Kimura. Everything I just told you is in Kimura's report. What he hasn't been able to work out is how the murderer got out of the building without being stopped. I thought I'd like to see the layout for myself."

He stood up and crossed to the bathroom. It had a small window high in the wall, no more than eighteen inches square, with frosted glass. Kicking off his shoes, Otani stood on the rim of the bath and reached up to open it. The

6

window was constructed so as to admit of its being opened only a few inches, and gave on to a blank wall about two feet away. Otani knew that the frame had been tested for fingerprints on the night of the murder, and that none had been found. If the murderer had dismantled the locking mechanism, and had been agile enough to get out that way, he would have needed an accomplice inside the hotel to put the window to rights again afterwards, in which case he ought to have been able to arrange just as easily to walk out of the main entrance.

He stepped down, and returned to the bed. A wood-and-paper shoji screen behind it gave the appearance of concealing a window, but when Otani slid it to one side nothing but rough plaster was revealed. Hanae looked up at him as he shuffled back across the bed on his knees, and he paused and touched her cheek. She smiled. "It's strange," she said. "In all these years I've listened to you thinking about cases often enough, but I don't think I've ever actually seen you behaving like a detective on television before."

Otani stepped down from the bed. "You are extremely privileged," he said loftily, then looked round the room again. "Really no natural light at all," he murmured. Round the ceiling were concealed fluorescent lights which glowed a sickly pink, while the bathroom was more brightly illuminated. "Switch on the beside light, would you?" he asked, and after trying the switches and at one point plunging the room into almost total darkness Hanae found the right one. "Now turn off the main room lights again," he commanded.

Hanae did so, and lay back, her face in shadow. "Very seductive," Otani commented. "I wonder if any light shows through the curtain." He pulled it across, and stood back. Only the dimmest glow penetrated the material, and he walked back to the door and switched on the room lights again.

7

Hanae's face appeared round the edge of the curtain. "I don't see the point of the curtain anyway," she said.

"A boy persuades his girl to come to a hotel for the first time," Otani said to the disembodied face of his wife. "They're both shy, but she's shyer than he is. So she retreats behind the curtain to undress, while he stays out here. Same again afterwards. Simple."

Hanae emerged, and stood beside Otani. "Yes, I suppose so," she said. "I wonder who on earth chooses the furnishings? It's an awful colour." She lifted the material to examine it, then turned it back to see the hem. "Very clumsily made up," she commented, then fingered a lump in the hem. "Look, they even left a cotton reel in it." Then her expression changed. "No, it's something else. I wonder what it can be?"

Otani took the bunched material from her. It was a synthetic furnishing fabric featuring bold lozenges of blue and pink, and Otani pulled the rough hemstitching open and peered into the pocket which resulted. Then he delved inside with thumb and forefinger and pulled out a carved ivory object about two inches long. They looked at it in silence for a moment, then Hanae took it from him. "How odd. It's a netsuke," she said.

Otani nodded. "Yes. A funny one, though. Not the sort you see in antique shops. It seems to be a carving of some sort of goddess. Bring it over to the table where there's more light."

"It seems to be quite old," said Hanae as they both contemplated the tiny statue, which incorporated a shallow circular base. The ivory had the brownish-yellow patina of age, and was worn smooth at its points of protuberance. The most marked of these were the disproportionately jutting breasts of the female figure depicted in flowing robes, the meticulously carved fingers of the hands, and the features of the face.

"It's not Buddhist, that's certain," said Otani. "Chinese, perhaps?"

Hanae shook her head in disagreement, and picked up the carving for a closer look. "No. Look, there's nothing Chinese about those robes. It might be copied from some Indian sculpture. Don't their goddesses have those huge breasts?"

"Don't ask me," said Otani. "You know I have no interest whatever in breasts." He winked expansively and eyed Hanae, whose own were unusually generous for a Japanese woman and who knew how her husband delighted in them.

She closed her eyes and shook her head in exasperation, then opened them again. "Well," she said, "what are we going to do? Put it back where we found it, or hand it in downstairs?"

Otani became serious. "Neither, I think," he said after a moment's thought. "It's obviously old, and might be valuable. If it is, we ought to try to identify it before asking the hotel management how they account for its being there. You never know, we might have a lost property claim form for it on the file at headquarters. I think I'll take charge of it for the moment." He took the carving from Hanae and fingered it gently.

"You don't think it could have anything to do with the murder, do you?" said Hanae, and Otani smiled.

"Hardly," he said, and slipped the netsuke into his jacket pocket. "It has very likely been there ever since the curtains were put up in the first place. Nevertheless, I shall be interested to find out a bit more about it."

He looked at his watch. "We've been here about forty-five minutes," he announced. "I should think we could go now without surprising them too much. We're entitled to two hours, but they'll probably assume I'm a business man taking a late lunch hour, and that you have to get home before your children get back from school."

He stood up and extended his hands to Hanae, who rose to her feet as well. She looked down demurely. "It seems

9

a waste of money not to make use of the room,'' she murmured, then put her arms around his neck.

Otani's expression softened yet again. ''You never stop amazing me,'' he said, and kissed her lightly. ''Splendid. Back behind the curtain with you. I've told you what to do.''

Chapter II

"**M**IGISHIMA," SAID INSPECTOR JIRO KIMURA patiently, gazing up at the burly young man looming over him in his tiny office at the headquarters of Hygo Prefectural Police near the harbour in Kobe. "I've told you before. There's not the slightest point in wearing plain clothes if you still look exactly like a policeman."

Patrolman Kenichi Migishima coloured uncomfortably, but stood his ground. "Sir," he said woodenly. He was wearing a perfectly ordinary mass-produced suit and a neat tie with his dazzling white shirt, in sharp contrast to his superior, who lolled back in his chair in a cashmere sweater, elegantly cut brown slacks and suede shoes.

Kimura, at forty, worked to keep his lean frame in good shape, and was discovering to his great satisfaction that as the years went by his saturnine good looks seemed to be as much of a help as ever in warding off any slackening of the pace of his exuberant love life. "I suppose it's not really the clothes, it's the way you move," he continued in a kindly but patronising manner. "Of course you have to go on thinking like a police officer now that you've joined my section, but try not to think like a *uniformed patrolman*, if you see what I mean.''

''Sir,'' said Migishima again, and with a visible effort of will achieved a slight effect of relaxation. Kimura sighed gently. ''Good,'' he said unconvincingly. ''Just go through it again, would you?''

Migishima turned his attention to the document attached to the clipboard he was holding in one large hand. ''The immigration people at Osaka airport were as helpful as possible, sir,'' he said. ''We checked back from the tourist visa entry in her passport and they were able to look up her landing card. If she had been younger they might have been suspicious, but she *was* thirty-seven. There's a note on the landing card to say that she was well-dressed and had plenty of travellers' cheques.''

Kimura leaned back and laced his fingers together. ''Interesting.'' he murmured. ''Filipino, single, occupation given as teacher. I think I'd have been suspicious. They don't pay teachers all that well in the Philippines, I should imagine.''

''There was a further note, sir,'' Migishima pressed on doggedly. ''It seems she stated that she was divorced. Then again, she gave her address in Japan as care of Kobe YWCA. A genuine teacher might easily want to stay there instead of a hotel.''

Kimura smiled, then sat up with an air of brisk efficiency. ''Well, it's a start. We must obviously find out more about this Miss Ventura of ours. I doubt if we shall get much help from the Philippine Consulate General, even though they are just up the road from where the woman was killed. I didn't get the impression they were disposed to do more than report the thing back to Manila in a routine way.'' He stood, and meticulously smoothed his sweater over his neat waist, then took a suede jacket carefully from a hanger on the wall behind him and slipped it on.

Migishima cleared his throat with elephantine delicacy. ''Er, instructions, sir?'' he said.

Kimura waved airily. "I'm going down to the YWCA," he announced. "I think it might be a good idea for you to dig about a little and find out who owns the Fantasia Hotel. Then ask Inspector Noguchi which gang branch it connects up with. It's bound to be one of them."

Migishima's face registered stark horror. "I am to ask Inspector Noguchi myself, sir?" he stammered, and Kimura pulled a face at him.

"Yes, you are to ask him yourself. He likes you, Migishima." Then he ducked out of the room and left his assistant to his misery.

It was a delightful morning, and Kimura hummed tunelessly to himself as he strolled jauntily among the shoppers thronging the area west of Sannomiya Station. The last of the year's typhoons had bypassed western Japan, but had brought in its wake the high blue skies of November. He pondered briefly which of his current panel of girlfriends he might invite for an outing to Kyoto to see the maple leaves in all their fiery glory. Very few of them were Japanese, but they of course would appreciate the romantic connotations more than the American and European secretaries he cultivated with such diligence. Some of these teased him about the ambiguity of his resounding title of Head of the Foreign Residents' Liaison Section, but the job certainly gave him access to most of the foreign girls working in the prefecture, and after all, the Hyogo Prefectural Police *were* the third largest force in Japan . . .

He knew where the YWCA was—unlike Superintendent Otani, he also knew what the initials stood for. Though Kimura was, as always, optimistic when approaching any environment with a strongly feminine aspect, he scarcely expected an atmosphere of languid sensuousness. He was, nevertheless, taken aback by the look of acute distaste on the pugnacious face of Miss Chieko Fukuda when he entered her office at the back of the reception area to one side of the entrance hall. It had been a little like going into

13

school anyway, and Miss Fukuda was like a headmistress in a nightmare. She was small yet burly, looking a little like one of the animated parcels on Post Office notices urging people to use correct addresses; but without the winsomeness of feature customary in such cartoons.

Spinsters are comparatively rare in Japan, and possibly for that very reason tend to be formidable. Miss Fukuda's evident hostility to what Kimura assumed was the entire male sex was of Olympic quality. "We have nothing to do with the police here," she announced grimly as Kimura was half-way into the room and the young girl receptionist who had escorted him there bolted for cover. Miss Fukuda's grey hair was cut short, and she was dressed in what Kimura at first took to be some kind of uniform but later concluded must be a plain jacket and skirt of dark blue serge.

She stood, with feet planted firmly apart, in front of her small desk as though to conceal the papers on its surface from her unwelcome visitor, and stared at Kimura with slightly pop-eyed intensity. Kimura had a generous abstract affection for all women in principle, and invariably tried to charm (even, on occasion, in a completely disinterested way) any member of the sex he encountered. Quite without conscious thought he paused, bowed very low and apologised in the most ceremonious manner for intruding. As cliché followed cliché Miss Fukuda's expression of implacable hatred gradually changed into one of simple contempt, and she heaved an ostentatiously patient sigh which made the silver crucifix pinned to the lapel of her jacket wink in the light from the fluorescent fixture above her head. Although the sun was bright outside, there was little evidence of the fact in the office, whose single window was covered with a lace curtain and which in any case gave on to a narrow alley between the YWCA and the neighbouring building.

Miss Fukuda cleared her throat. "Yes," she agreed coldly. "It would have been better for you to make an

14

appointment, if you really had to see me. Now, what is it you want?''

Kimura philosophically accepted failure in his role of male charmer, and adopted the stance of a senior police officer with no time to waste, either. He produced his official identity card and flashed it at Miss Fukuda as he had seen it done many times in the TV Serials imported from America and dubbed for Japanese TV. She gave no indication of having noticed. ''Kimura, Inspector, Hyogo Prefectural Police,'' he said briskly. ''Enquiring into the circumstances of the death of a Filipino national. I should like to examine your register of residents for the past few months of this year.''

This announcement did cause Miss Fukuda to lose some of her composure, and the square body sagged a little. ''*What* did you say?''

''Murder, I'm afraid,'' Kimura continued, all antiseptic efficiency, and this time Miss Fukuda's mouth opened and the protuberant eyes widened.

''You mean . . . one of our ladies . . . ?''

Kimura nodded. ''Well, possibly,'' he said. ''She gave this address on her landing card, but that was four months ago. And of course she may never have come here at all. Her name was Ventura. Cleo Ventura.''

As soon as she heard the name Miss Fukuda's mouth tightened again, and the look of disapproval was back on her face. ''Miss Ventura,'' she said, and nodded heavily. ''So Miss Ventura has been murdered, you say?''

Kimura was beginning to find Miss Fukuda's froglike appearance depressing. ''If I may say so, you sound neither surprised nor particularly sorry,'' he said with a certain stiffness. ''Evidently you do remember her.''

Miss Fukuda hastily adjusted her features into an appearance of Christian resignation. ''I am deeply distressed,'' she conceded. ''I do not remember Miss Ventura very well. Most of our guests are of course foreign. It is

15

unusual for us to welcome anyone from the Philippines, though. They are nearly all Catholics, you know.''

Kimura had only the sketchiest understanding of Western religion and not much more of Buddhism or Shinto, but he nodded with every appearance of scholarly interest. ''Of course,'' he agreed.

''She stayed only a few days, I think,'' Miss Fukuda went on, and struck a small bell on the desk behind her with the palm of one pudgy hand.

Almost at once the young receptionist opened the door and peeped in. ''The register,'' Miss Fukuda intoned, and the face disappeared. A male voice could be heard outside, and Kimura was interested to see a look of syrupy adoration appear on Miss Fukuda's face, and a distinct crimsoning of her sallow skin. He had little time to speculate, because the door was now flung wide and a tall, bony foreigner entered, rising and falling exaggeratedly from the ankles with each step.

The athleticism of the man's movements gave Kimura the impression of having been added as a conscious embellishment of his normal manner. Being extraordinarily attentive to his own image, he was quick to recognise the trait in others, and he noted and filed away his conclusion in no more than the time it took for Miss Fukuda to cry out gladly in greeting. ''Mr Goober! What a delightful surprise!'' Kimura's own English was so fluent and relaxed that it was not until Mr Goober replied that he realised that Miss Fukuda had in fact switched to that language.

Mr Goober's thin, almost tragic face creased into a practised beam which embraced both the Japanese. ''Chieko-san,'' he said, to Kimura's great interest. Given names are rarely used in Japan except in the case of young children, and even though he was habituated to the particular enthusiasm of Americans for intimate forms of address, it was a jolt to hear the formidable Miss Fukuda referred to in that way. ''It's *good* to see you.'' Mr Goober gave to the cliché a weight and conviction of utterance which might have

16

been more appropriate if he had at last announced his conclusion after summing up an immensely complex sequence of scientific reasoning.

Then he gave his fullest attention to Kimura and began to speak to him in the most abominable Japanese. Kimura allowed him to get no more than partially into his first sentence of introduction before cutting in. "Hello, Mr Goober," he said, sticking out his hand amiably. "As a matter of fact, I do speak a little English. My name's Jiro Kimura. Inspector, Hyogo Prefectural Police."

Mr Goober, who had been virtually on balletic points till then, slowly subsided until his feet were at last planted firmly in one place. "I'll be darned," he said folksily. It was not clear whether he was expressing amazement at Kimura's command of English or at his station in life. He had retained possession of Kimura's hand and now began to pump it. "Reverend Willard Goober. It's good to meet you, Inspector. What can we do for you, sir?"

Kimura retrieved his hand with some difficulty and put it decisively in his pocket. "As a matter of fact, Mr Goober, I was in conference with Miss Fukuda here," he said pointedly.

Mr Goober turned to Miss Fukuda for confirmation, rising to his toes again as he did so. Kimura noticed that his shoes were extremely dirty, and so old as to be almost falling apart. Miss Fukuda gazed idiotically into the missionary's eyes. "The Inspector was asking about one of our residents, Mr Goober," she sighed girlishly.

Mr Goober wheeled back to Kimura, who had decided that it was high time he regained the upper hand. He spoke in a firm, official manner. "Mr Goober, I am here on police business. I am calling on Miss Fukuda as General Secretary of the YWCA. May I ask what is your status here? I don't recall your name as being on my file of foreign residents."

Mr Goober paid no attention to the question, but looked searchingly into Kimura's black diamond eyes. "You need

17

inner peace, my friend," he said kindly, nodding slowly. "Will you allow me to help you to come to the Lord?" Kimura never admitted to being flummoxed in dealing with foreigners, frequently claiming to Superintendent Otani over beer and *sushi* that Westerners at least should be handled as though dealing with a very small child telling fibs. Mr Goober's approach was distinctly disconcerting, however, and he stepped back a little and looked him up and down to give himself time.

The American was a good six inches taller than Kimura, who was of average height for a Japanese of his generation, but tightly muscular in build. Goober was perhaps in his late thirties, and had big bones of the type that seem to be on the point of bursting through the skin surface. His hair looked to be of a sandy colour, but was cropped so short that it might have been greying near the large pink ears.

He was wearing a shabby brown suit with arms and legs too short for him, a shirt with a collar which Kimura could see was badly frayed, and a tie with a knot tied so tightly that it was little larger than a fair-sized haricot bean. It looked to Kimura as though Goober must have devised some method of putting the tie on and taking it off so that the knot remained undisturbed. Or perhaps he slept in it. When Otani used to tease him about his un-Japanese partiality for the company of foreigners, Kimura would usually deny that they smelt all that bad. Indeed he found the characteristic mixture of perfume and femininity about American and European women extremely attractive. But there was no doubt whatever that Goober gave off a disagreeable odour. Miss Fukuda's room had when Kimura first entered it been filled with the scent of a powerfully perfumed furniture polish, but this was now overlaid by a reminiscence of old biscuits which could only be emanating from Mr Goober, who now produced a well-thumbed book from his pocket. It fell open as if by Divine intervention.

"In my Father's house are many mansions," he read,

then looked up. "Many mansions, Jiro. May I call you Jiro?"

Kimura was outraged. "No, Mr Goober, you may not," he barked. "I asked you a question. What is your status here?"

Mr Goober was immersed in his New Testament again and made no response, so Kimura glared at Miss Fukuda. Clearly besotted as she was with the American, she remained Japanese enough to react to the authority in Kimura's voice, and replied in their own language. "Mr Goober is a pastor working in the poorest part of Osaka," she said. "He conducts several Bible classes for us each week here, and we are deeply in debt to him." Then she raised her chin defiantly, her face now deeply flushed. "Mr Goober meant no offence to you, Inspector. He spoke merely for your good. American people prefer to use our given names."

At this point Mr Goober joined in, his English as flat as the plains in Oklahoma. "Yup. Know what General Booth said? 'Go for souls, and go for the worst.' That's my motto too." The smile again split his pale Buster Keaton mask of gloom, and he wagged his head at Kimura.

Kimura experienced a sensation of going under, and addressed himself again to Miss Fukuda. "I shall inspect the register outside," he muttered. "I am sorry to have intruded. If we have further questions for you I will make an appointment."

Clearly Mr Goober understood the Japanese word for "appointment", because as Kimura stiffly made his exit he zoomed up to the tip-toe position again and flung his arms wide. The New Testament flew from his outstretched hand and knocked over a green glass vase containing sprays of miniature chrysanthemums which was standing on Miss Fukuda's desk. She made for it with a small moan. "Remember your appointment with the Lord, friend," the nasal voice insisted to Kimura's retreating back. "The Men's

19

Scripture Study and Spiritual Awareness Group meet at the other Y. Wednesdays, six p.m. Open your heart, Jiro—''

Kimura shut the door behind him with unnecessary force, and met the eyes of the young receptionist, who was clutching what must be the register to her small bosom. ''I'll look at it out here,'' he said to her with relief, gently prising the book from her grasp. He took it over to the counter and began turning over the leaves. ''Is he always like that?'' he enquired without looking up.

There was no reply, so he glanced over his shoulder at the girl. She was nodding dumbly, her eyes wide, and Kimura grinned. He suddenly felt much better, and resumed his scrutiny of the register, with part of his mind wondering what Miss Fukuda and Mr Goober were talking about behind the closed door of her office. Profound though her passion obviously was, it was difficult to envision her in his bony embrace.

There it was, two days after the date on the landing card. Cleo Ventura, of Manila. Miss Fukuda had been right. Mrs Ventura seemed to have checked out a bare five days after her arrival, but she had given a forwarding address. Kimura jotted it down. Evidently she had gone to stay with a compatriot. Fuentes was another Filipino name, he knew. Kimura had over two hundred Filipino residents in his parish; they were one of the largest national groups after, of course, the Koreans, the Chinese, Indians, Americans and British. Kimura paid small attention to the first three groups, preferring to leave their routine supervision to his subordinates and to turn more serious matters over to his colleague Noguchi of the Drugs Section. Noguchi seemed not to mind hobnobbing with them, and even admitted to having cronies among the Koreans.

He closed his notebook and put it away, then handed the register back to the receptionist just as the swing doors on the opposite side of the entrance hall swung open and a group of about a dozen Japanese ladies came out, gossiping animatedly among themselves. To Kimura's experienced eye all were in the mid-thirties or older, and all were quite plainly in comfortable financial circumstances. A few were dressed in expensive-looking kimonos, while most of the others seemed to run to Gucci handbags, cashmere sweaters and imported silk scarves.

Kimura never minded being the focus of female attention, and he preened himself happily under the speculative scrutiny of so many pairs of eyes. Then all at once one of the ladies broke away from the group heading for the door and he realised that it was Mrs Otani, of all people. She was one of those in kimono, and he had rarely seen her in traditional dress. She bowed rather shyly, and he hastily returned her greeting. "It is a long time since we have met," she murmured in the conventional phrase, and he responded with the appropriate enquiries about her health and that of her husband, in whose company he had in fact been until about an hour and half previously.

The preliminaries completed, Hanae stood back and surveyed Kimura. In all the years during which he had worked so closely with Otani, Hanae had met him no more than a dozen or so times, but Otani grumbled about him so frequently at home that she felt she knew him well. She had developed a very soft spot for him over the years, and though she tut-tutted whenever Otani made some reference to the inspector's dedicated efforts to live up to the *Playboy* ideal of the sophisticated urban male's sex life, she was secretly quite intrigued, just as she strongly suspected Otani was, too.

She permitted herself a twinkle at him as she looked him in the eye. "What a surprise to see you here, Kimura-san! I wouldn't have expected you to have any lady friends at the YWCA."

He grinned cheerfully. "That's because I never thought I could hope for such a pleasant encounter as this," he said, his automatically flirtatious gallantry infused with real warmth and pleasure. "If I may ask, what brings you here today?"

21

Hanae pointed to the notice board on which were displayed details of the timetables of classes. "I come here once a week for a cookery lesson. I am studying what they call *cordon blue*."

Kimura looked at her kimono, beautifully smooth and perfect, its heavy cream silk splashed with autumnal russets and browns. "In that lovely kimono?" he asked, and she smiled.

"Not usually," she said. "Today was just a talk, no demonstration. We generally dress up rather on lecture days." Hanae did indeed look the very picture of Japanese elegance, composed, mature and dignified, her tranquil face gentle and unblemished, her lips perhaps a little too full for classic Japanese beauty, but extremely attractive all the same. She looked quizzically at Kimura. "Problems? You seem to be very busy." It was a euphemism for "flustered", and they both knew it.

Kimura ruefully scratched his head in a gesture which is thought by Japanese to exude boyish charm. "I have had rather a trying interview with the General Secretary," he admitted. "Does Madam have a few minutes to spare for a cup of coffee? I feel as if I need one."

Hanae instantly blushed, and thought furiously. Kimura was an old acquaintance, who always scrupulously addressed her as "Madam". Their encounter was completely accidental, and what harm could there possibly be in a cup of coffee? She would, needless to say, tell Tetsuo all about it that very evening. On the other hand, this was the first time she had ever been alone with him, and he *did* have a terrible reputation . . . but it *would* be agreeable to sit and chat for a while over a cup of coffee . . . It took her no more than a few seconds to make up her mind. "Thank you. I should enjoy that." She smiled again, and glanced defiantly at two of her classmates who were lingering in the entrance, transparent in their attempts to conceal that they were watching the scene with avidity.

Kimura hadn't really expected Hanae to take up his offer, and found to his own surprise that her acceptance made him feel distinctly elated. He ushered her to the door and they stepped out into the sunshine. He pointed to the opposite side of the street. "Over there. 'Coffee New Monaco.' It looks quite alright," he said, and daringly took Hanae's elbow to escort her across.

Chapter III

OTANI SUPPOSED THAT HE REALLY OUGHT TO HAVE made an appointment at the National Museum of Kyoto through the Kyoto prefectural force, but reasoned that he had come by the netsuke in his personal and private capacity: very personal, and very private, indeed. It was a simple question of finding some knowledgeable person on the staff there to give him a rough idea of the age of the thing and say whether it might be of any particular value.

It was always agreeable to come to Kyoto during the autumn, and he sniffed the crisp air appreciatively as he emerged from the Keihan Railway terminus at Sanjo and glanced at the northern hills, with the Chinese character for "Great" carved boldly on the hillside high above the Temple of the Silver Pavilion in clear view not much more than a mile or so away. A pity they had missed the Daimonji Festival yet again. One August before long he and Hanae would book a room at one of the hotels near the Kamo River and watch from the roof garden as the fires were lit one after the other and the Buddhist messages of farewell to the spirits of the departed flared out on the five wooded

24

hills to mark the conclusion of their annual visit to the presence of the living.

Otani couldn't remember how far it was to the Museum, and set out boldly to walk there via Okazaki and Maruyama Park. At least the geometrically laid-out streets of Kyoto made it difficult to lose one's way, though one did tend to forget what a big sprawling city it was.

An hour later Otani was sitting up at the counter of a small restaurant eating the last of his tempura lunch, reassured to learn that he was quite near his destination. It had been pleasant sitting there watching the elderly cook-proprietor dipping morsels of chicken, sliced onion and lily root, two whole prawns, an aromatic *shiso* leaf and other tit-bits into the light batter and frying them for a few moments in the deep vat of golden oil with its protective hood, then placing them one by one on the sheet of absorbent paper on its delicate woven bamboo tray in front of Otani, keeping easy pace with him as he ate. The old man was chatty after the custom of his profession, and his Kyoto accent was quaint but naïve, unlike the affected fluting refinement of many of the snobbish middle- and upper-class products of the city whom Otani had met in his time.

After the last mouthful of rice, the last piece of pungent pickled radish which enabled him to agree with sincerity with the proprietor that Kyoto *takuan* really was the best in Japan. Otani paid his eight hundred and fifty yen, drained his beaker of green tea and made his way through the divided short curtain at the sliding wood-and-paper door with a last word of farewell.

It was as the old chap had said. Otani had only to walk for another five minutes to find himself at the spacious junction of Number Seven Street and the Great Eastern Avenue. The Museum was to his right and across the broad street was the parking area of the Sanjusangendo Temple. Otani paused to watch, without a great deal of interest, a tourist bus spew out a party of middle-aged foreigners,

25

festooned with cameras and airline bags, and got up, to his eye, in the most extraordinary garb.

Otani found the clothes of many of the younger generation of Japanese pretty outlandish, but only on the one occasion when for some unfathomable but no doubt deeply political reason Ambassador Tsunematsu of the Foreign Ministry liaison office in Osaka had pressed him to visit a hideously expensive golf club in his company had Otani seen numbers of his own countrymen of about his own age in such lurid checked trousers, pastel-coloured sports shirts and silly hats. The women looked slightly less absurd, but the hubbub of their shrill voices was audible even from Otani's quite distant vantage point, and he turned his back on the scene, wishing them well of the celebrated array of one thousand and one images of Kannon. Privately he considered them boring and overpraised.

There were foreigners in evidence inside the Museum too, but for some reason it seemed to attract a more sober, scholarly type of visitor, and in any case the overwhelming majority of the people wandering around the spacious galleries were Japanese.

Having studied the plan of the Museum's layout in the entrance hall, Otani had no trouble in making his way to the gallery which housed the collection of netsuke. Since this entailed his departing from the recommended route, Otani attracted a number of censorious glances from the more conservative visitors and attendants.

There must have been over a hundred of the intricate little carvings on display, and Otani for a while almost forgot why he had come, so absorbed did he become in the wit, humour and imagination which had so obviously gone into their creation. There were mythical figures and Chinese priests and hermits by the dozen; fearsome skulls with serpents emerging from the eye-sockets, comical turtles, rabbits and other bravura feats of carving like a piece of ivory turned into a tiny bamboo cage containing what looked like a perfect sphere. Otani shook his head slowly, wondering at the paradox that these delicate works of art had for the most part served the very humble everyday purpose of toggles for tobacco pouches.

Then he looked around and saw on the wall a large notice in closely-written script giving an account of the origins of netsuke and drawing attention to some of the choicer items in the Museum's collection. He read it attentively, absent-mindedly fondling the little piece of ivory in his trouser pocket, then stood completely motionless for several seconds as he came to one sentence which he re-read several times.

After that Otani looked around him thoughtfully. The only person in any kind of apparent authority was an elderly attendant sitting on a folding chair in the corner by the doorway, so Otani approached her. She looked up at him amiably enough as he apologised for bothering her. "I was just reading about the netsuke," he explained, "where it says that there are hardly any examples of representations of foreign people."

"Except Chinese, of course," the old lady said in an unexpectedly educated voice. "Lots of Chinese figures. You mean barbarians, I suppose." She used the old word for Westerners quite unselfconsciously, and Otani found himself warming to her rapidly.

"Well, now, what about the set of figures that are supposed to be National Treasures? Where are they on show?"

She shook her head, the old eyes bright among the wrinkles. "Just once a year for the special exhibition," she said. "The set is incomplete, you see." She rummaged through a pile of catalogues on a small shelf beside her chair. "I've seen them several times, of course," she muttered. "They often ask me to move to a different room, but I like the netsuke. Let me see now." She found what she was looking for and opened an illustrated booklet, turning the pages slowly and stopping from time to time as a picture caught her eye. Otani waited patiently until she offered him the catalogue, pointing out one photograph.

27

It was one of those rare moments which had come to him at long intervals during his police career, when what had seemed like an idle and almost frivolous initiative was crowned with a bit of pure and unadulterated luck. There on the page was a reproduction of a subtly illuminated colour photograph of a group of seven ivory netsuke, differing from each other in detail, but exhibiting an obvious family resemblance. And there could be no doubt whatever that he had in his pocket an eighth member of the family.

"Strange, aren't they?" The attendant was looking up at him quizzically, and it was with an effort that Otani refocused his attention upon her, smiled politely and handed the catalogue back.

"Interesting, though" he commented. "I'd really like to come and see them next time they're put on show. Thank you very much." He bowed, she bowed, and Otani made his way to the main entrance, with a last glance at the netsuke display cases as he passed them.

The Director was absent on official business, and the Curator was extremely uneasy about receiving Otani in his absence. He was a thin, abstracted-looking man who must have been approaching retiring age, and he sat on the edge of a chair in the Director's reception room turning Otani's visiting card over and over with long, nervous fingers as Otani apologised for asking for an interview without an appointment. The Curator's collar was several sizes too big for him, and his clothing remained as immobile as a suit of armour while he seemed to twitch and writhe within it.

With gentle patience Otani explained that he had come to the Museum as an ordinary visitor and had been particularly struck by the netsuke. The attendant had been kind enough to show him a photograph of an unusual set of examples which were only rarely on display, being designated as National Treasures.

At last the expert began to relax a little. "You mean the Muses."

Otani nodded, having no idea what the foreign word the man was using could mean. "I should be very interested to know why they are so highly prized," he said with an air of complete comprehension.

The Curator was a much more impressive person when launched fairly on his own subject, and he spoke with increasing ease and authority. "Well, you see, the whole matter of netsuke is extraordinarily interesting," he began, "and the history of this particular set is highly unusual." He paused and gave Otani a schoolmasterly look of interrogation. "You are, I take it, familiar with the history of our country during the period of exclusion from foreign contacts?"

Otani spread his hands deprecatingly. "Well, of course I know it lasted two hundred years or so, and that nobody was allowed to enter or leave Japan."

The other man pursed his dry lips. "That is broadly correct," he acknowledged. "However, contact with the rest of the world was not totally cut off. From the middle of the seventeenth century until the Americans came with their Black Ships in 1854 the Dutchmen were allowed to keep their small trading post on Dejima island in Nagasaki harbour, and to bring one shipload of cargo to Japan each year."

Otani nodded. "Yes, of course. I recall lessons in my schooldays about what was called 'Dutch Studies' in those days. A few Japanese scholars were allowed to learn their language, weren't they?"

This time the Curator nodded, in benign approval. "Just so. Well, you may also recall that one of the conditions imposed upon the Dutch traders was that each year their leader was required to make the long journey to Kyoto and thence along the Tokaido road—the fifty-three stages—to Tokyo, or Edo as it was then, of course, to pay homage to the Shogun in Edo Castle. And, needless to say, to bring costly presents."

"And these were a present from the Dutch to the Shogun?" In his excitement Otani butted in, and was crushed by a withering glance from the Curator, who continued his exposition.

"The presents were, of course, usually of European manufacture. Guns it might be, or clocks and other instruments. It seems that round about the middle of the eighteenth century, when netsuke were in common use among the samurai classes, the incumbent head of the Dutch trading post hit upon the idea of having a local Japanese craftsman carve a set of netsuke depicting the nine Greek Muses."

That word again, coupled with a reference to Greece which Otani *did* understand. His attempts to conceal his ignorance must have been unsuccessful, for a brief smile flitted across the expert's desiccated lips. "Nine sister goddesses," he explained. "Each the patron of one particular art or science. We do not know the name of the craftsman who carved them, but one thing is quite certain. He could never have set eyes on a European woman. The foreigners were not permitted to bring their own women with them, and were provided with female companions from among local women of the humbler courtesan class. So he must have depended on verbal descriptions or perhaps crude sketches drawn by the Dutchmen." The thin lips twitched again. "The Japanese carver must have been particularly persuaded that Greek goddesses had very large breasts, and long noses. The work is technically accomplished, but the figures are voluptuous to the point of fantasy."

Surreptitiously, Otani slid his hand into his pocket and fingered his personal goddess. The protuberances were indeed noticeable.

"At all events, the gift must have pleased the Shogun of the time, and no doubt the Dutch Agent-General received favours as a result. A reference to the set of nine netsuke appears in an inventory of Tokugawa family treasures made in the year 1758, and they were listed again at intervals up to just before the fall of the Tokugawa shogunate and the restoration of the Meiji Emperor a hundred or so years ago.''

The Curator had closed his eyes, confident of Otani's full attention. ''We do not know precisely what became of them for a long time after that. There is no record of their sale or transfer by way of gift, but somehow or other seven of them came into th. ossesion of General Yago.''

''Not the Yago who was tried as a war criminal at the same time as Tojo and the others?''

This time Otani's interruption seemed not to give offence, and the Curator opened his eyes and nodded. ''Yes. Yago was sentenced to ten years' imprisonment, was released after a good deal less than that on medical grounds, and died . . . let me see, some time in the early sixties, it would have been. The General had been a great collector, and all his assets beyond a modest provision for his wife were confiscated at the time of his conviction. Quite a lot of his possessions were placed in the national museums, but very few were important enough to be designated as National Treasures. Of course, once the netsuke were identified as the ones presented to the forme Shogun we had little difficulty in resisting the Yago family's attempts to challenge the confiscation.''

Otani's eyes rose in genuine surprise at the turn the story was taking, and the Curator reverted briefly to his former nervous manner. ''Naturally,'' he stammered, ''I should not reveal these, ah, legal details if you were not a senior police officer . . .''

Otani hastened to reassure him. ''I am most grateful to you,'' he said. ''I shall of course regard what you have told me as confidential. The fact is, I was less than candid with you earlier. You say that Yago had only seven of the nine pieces in his possession?''

The Curator heaved a sigh and nodded mournfully. ''I fear that the other two must have been irretrievably lost. There has never been any suggestion that the former General ever had the complete set.''

31

Otani could not resist the impulse which came upon him, and he produced his netsuke. "Could this be one of the other two?" he asked blandly, and set the little figure on the table between them.

He regretted his action almost at once, though the effect it had on the Curator was certainly startling enough. He sat stock still for a while, then made several unsuccessful attempts to find his voice. Finally he reached out with a trembling hand and picked up the netsuke. "How . . . *how* did you come by this?" His voice was still barely under control, and he was gazing at the netsuke as though hypnotised, waves of colour drifting across his thin features.

"There's no doubt in your mind?" As he asked the question Otani reached across and retrieved the netsuke, which the Curator clutched at too late.

"None whatever," the expert replied, a wary look coming into his eyes. "There will of course need to be a full investigation. The Director—and of course the Agency for Cultural Affairs—will be overjoyed to know that one at least of our missing National Treasures has been restored."

The shutters closed over Otani's face and he slipped the carving back into his pocket. "I don't quite follow you," he said quietly. "The netsuke I have in my possession has not been designated as a National Treasure. Nor is it so far as I am aware the property of the State. It is for the police to determine the legal owner. In due course the Museum authorities will be advised of our findings." He stood up, and the Curator followed suit, his mouth partly open.

For a moment Otani had the feeling that he was about to fight for the possession of the carving. Then the Curator drew himself up with a good deal of dignity. "Do I understand you to imply that you refuse to leave the netsuke in the custody of the Museum?"

Otani nodded. "You do," he agreed.

"You assume a heavy responsibility, Superintendent," said the Curator, his voice rather unsteady. "I am in no doubt whatever that the courts will confirm the designation of the object as a National Treasure. As a police officer you should be aware that violation of the Cultural Property Protection Law is a serious offence, carrying a possible penalty of five years' imprisonment . . ."

Otani looked him up and down with a new respect. "I can understand your concern," he said. "Unfortunately, my interpretation of my duty is in conflict with your view of your own. The netsuke is for the moment to be regarded as a piece of evidence in a criminal investigation, and it therefore remains in police custody." The Curator's expression changed and the two men looked at each levelly. "I should be grateful if you would regard what I have just said as confidential. Meantime, I have one more question. You spoke a while ago of attempts by the Yago family to challenge the confiscation. Is the widow still alive?"

"No. She died soon after the former General. The head of the family is his son. With his connections as a member of the National Diet he is in a position to cause a considerable upheaval in official circles whenever he chooses. The last occasion was at least five years ago, though, and the courts refused to reopen the case."

Otani nodded thoughtfully, then bowed. "I am sorry to have intruded and to have taken up your valuable time," he apologised formally.

"Not at all," the expert replied. His manner was civil, but he was gazing fixedly in the direction of Otani's trouser pocket.

Chapter IV

Jiro Kimura and Ninja Noguchi made a strange couple as they approached the small apartment block called Kobe Heights Mansion, according to the phonetic script on the sign affixed to the outside wall. Kimura was as natty as ever, and swung along jauntily in the mild afternoon sunshine, his tweed sports jacket flapping open as he gesticulated to his companion. Although Inspector Noguchi was keeping up with Kimura without the least effort, he nevertheless gave the impression of shuffling along on flat feet. He looked as though he had slept in his wrinkled and baggy trousers, which were secured by an enormous leather belt with various brass fitments here and there. The upper half of his massive body was encased in a grubby shirt buttoned to the neck but worn without a tie, and a jacket which had obviously once belonged to a different suit from his trousers.

Noguchi was getting on for sixty and Otani fought a continuous and so far successful battle with the personnel people to defer the date of his retirement. As nominal head of the Drugs Section of the prefectural force, Noguchi spent far more time outside police headquarters than at his scruffy little desk on the ground floor, and as years went by seemed to retain all his legendary ability to melt into his surroundings, whether in the guise of a tout at the races, a workman on his way to do a job in some select residential area, or a day-labourer drinking cheap potato spirit in a tiny open-fronted bar. "You'll get nothing out of them," he rumbled irritably as Kimura glanced at the names on the letter-boxes at the foot of the open stairs.

"It's worth a try, Ninja," came the cheerful reply. "Look at this—practically every single one a foreigner."

"Except for *him*," said Noguchi, stabbing a finger at a Japanese name on one of the boxes, then spitting on the dusty asphalt before making for the stairs. "He'll have told them what to say and what not to say. Third floor."

"Thank you for coming along," Kimura said as he bounded up the narrow concrete stairs after Noguchi.

"Had to," Noguchi grunted. "Got to try to get it across to the organisation that we're not quarrelling with their ordinary rackets. They wouldn't trust you, lad. Besides, it might be interesting to see you taking on four at once."

Kimura sniffed with a touch of hauteur as they reached a metal door with the name "Thorndike" in Roman script painted on a small panel with the Japanese equivalent "Sondaiku" underneath. Kimura pressed the bell-push at the side of the door and they waited for what seemed some time before the door was opened a few inches, showing a safety chain in place.

"Miss Thorndike?" Kimura enquired breezily. It was difficult to see the person on the other side of the door, but the answer came readily enough.

"I'm Amanda Thorndike. Let me see your identification."

"Surely," said Kimura, raising an eyebrow towards Noguchi. He delved into his inside pocket and produced his identity card, which he held up to the gap. After a moment

35

the door was closed, they heard the chain rattle, and it was opened fully.

The door gave on to a small entryway no more than a metre square, which was littered with shoes. Amanda Thorndike was standing barefoot on the tatami matting just beyond it, a tall girl in jeans and a blue tee-shirt which clung to her breasts. Kimura already knew that she was twenty-six years old, and was, as so often, struck by the strength of character in this young Western woman's face compared with those of most Japanese girls of the same age.

Amanda Thorndike was quite obviously on guard. Her face was long and sardonic, her brown eyes hooded but intelligent, flicking from Kimura to Noguchi and back. "Beauty and the Beast," she murmured as if to herself. "Come on in, fuzz." She stood to one side as the two men stepped out of their shoes and up on to the tatami. Three other women were sprawled on cushions round a low table with a plastic surface made to resemble lacquer. Through an open *fusuma* screen could be seen a heap of untidy bedding in an adjoining six-mat room, while the main room, which was only slightly larger, gave on to a small kitchen with what must be bathroom beyond.

Noguchi inclined his bullet head in the general direction of the table, then made for a corner of the room and low-ered himself into a squatting position, saying nothing. "In-spector Noguchi," Kimura remarked brightly. "My name's Kimura. Thank you for agreeing to this meeting, ladies." He remained standing as Amanda Thorndike joined the group round the table, and surveyed them. "You must be Judy Cheng," he said to a girl with oriental features staring at an open can of Suntory beer on the table before her, and she nodded sullenly.

"From Taiwan," said Kimura. He transferred his gaze to the fragile, pretty girl with her back to the translucent paper shoji screen. Her hair was very pale blonde and was tied back with a scrap of green ribbon. Her eyes were grey
36

and enormous, and she looked extremely vulnerable. "Je crois que vous êtes Mademoiselle Hélène Dupré," said Kimura with something of a flourish. His accent was by no means bad, but nothing like as easy and natural as his English. An expression of mild surprise came into the big eyes, and the girl nodded slowly.

"Clever boy," said the fourth girl with what looked to Kimura uncommonly like a sneer. She had black hair cut short, a lively urchin face, and was the only one who was wearing make-up.

Kimura was nettled. "Thank you, Miss Nancy Bernstein," he said with heavy irony. "Personally, I think it a matter of simple courtesy to address people in their own language whenever possible."

Nancy grinned, more to herself than to Kimura. "Okay, mine's Yiddish," she said, the heavy New York accent obvious even to Kimura.

He made an irritated gesture, and turned his attention to Amanda. "May I sit down?"

"Feel free," she said, waving a long hand towards a spare cushion near the table. Noguchi remained completely silent as Amanda smiled in his direction. "Your friend is frightfully chatty," she said, the clipped British tones incongruous in the grubby little room.

"Inspector Noguchi will have something to say in due course, Miss Thorndike," Kimura said. "Mainly to Mr Nakayama when he joins us."

Amanda raised a well-plucked eyebrow. "Oh, I doubt if old Nackers will put in an appearance," she said. "I don't think he's seen the light of day since he left school."

Kimura looked at his electronic watch. He had been having a good deal of trouble with it but it had been keeping reasonable time for the past two or three days. "He has been asked to make himself available at three forty-five," he said. "It is now three ten. Roughly. In the next half an hour I should like to ask you some questions." He looked at the French girl. "You understand English?"

"Of course." The voice was husky. "You do not 'ave to worry."

Kimura felt a distinct frisson of pleasure and sternly cleared his throat. "Yes. Well, ladies, the reason we asked to see you here is because I should like first of all to explain what we are *not* investigating. I am of course fully aware that none of you is in possession of a work permit, but that you all nevertheless work as hostesses at the Love Box Cabaret here in Kobe. I give you my word that I have no intention of taking the matter up with immigration or tax authorities—in consideration of your cooperation in helping me with my enquiries into another matter entirely. Inspector Noguchi has already made this plain to Nakayama-san's employers, and will repeat it to Nakayama himself."

"Big. deal," said Nancy. "Might have supposed you fascists would keep dossiers on us *gaijin*."

Kimura stiffened. "I will pass over that remark just for the moment," he said. "Just bear in mind that I spoke in terms of cooperation, though."

"Simmer down, Nancy love," said Amanda. "Hear him out."

Kimura glanced at her with appreciation. "Thank you, Miss Thorndike. I repeat that there is no doubt in my mind that you are all earning money in Japan on an illegal basis, but that is not relevant to my present investigation. I think it unlikely that proceedings will be taken against any of you before you leave Japan."

"And just what makes you think we plan on leaving?"

Nancy's manner was almost as belligerent as before, and Kimura gazed at her coolly, assisted by the fact that he found her the least physically attractive of the four women.

"You may wish to begin considering such plans, Miss Bernstein," he said. "I have been doing this job for a number of years now. I have met quite a lot of people like you. The money is easy, but the way of life tends to lose its attractions after a while . . . just as people in your business tend to lose theirs. Most of you move on after a few

38

months. A few stay. One or two get into serious trouble. Like Cleo Ventura.''

Amanda's long, humorous face was still. ''Poor old Cleo,'' she said quietly.

''You all knew her, of course?'' As he looked at their faces in turn Kimura noticed with some surprise that large tears had welled up in Judy Cheng's eyes, and he addressed himself directly to her. ''She was a friend of yours, Miss Cheng?''

She sniffed, and spoke in the characteristic sing-song English which Kimura had noticed before in Taiwanese. ''Cleo was my friend. She was good to talk to.''

''How long had you known her? All the four months she was here?''

Judy shook her little head, and her glossy black bell of hair swayed with the movement. ''Two, three years,'' she said. ''First time in Japan. Yokohama. Then we go together Manila. Good business there. Then come back here.''

During this recital Kimura looked steadily at the girl, but Amanda was still in his field of vision and he thought he saw her make and quickly suppress a warning gesture. He nodded, and deliberately addressed himself to Hélène Dupré. ''Of course we knew that Cleo Ventura had been in Japan previously,'' he lied smoothly.

''Horse feathers,'' Nancy remarked.

Kimura turned to her heavily. ''Miss Bernstein, don't push your luck,'' he said. ''I'll tell you for the last time. What I'm concerned with is a murder, and *most* other things can stay on the shelf. If you go on needling me though, I'll run you out.''

''Don't worry, I'm splitting anyway,'' she almost snarled.

Against his better judgment Kimura joined battle with her. Something about her dark, angry expression constituted an irresistible challenge, though even as he reacted he began to regret it. There were altogether too many witnesses to his unprofessional irritation. "Finding it difficult to attract customers? I'm not surprised."

Nancy thumped her two hands as fists on the table, and Judy, her cheeks still streaked with tears, hastily moved her beer can. "Listen, smart-ass," Nancy began thickly, her voice barely under control, "don't think you fool us any. You *hate* gaijin, the whole damn hypocritical bunch of you. But you're pathetic. You drool and grunt over white boobs, and when your pants are down you'll hand over everything in your billfold to cop a feel."

"A shabby little island delighted with itself . . ." The amused, elegant voice of Amanda floated into the exchange, and Kimura spun round as though he had been stung. "Don't mind me, Inspector," she said calmly. "I was quoting what somebody once said about England. It just struck me that it applies rather well to Japan, too."

Kimura took a deep breath in preparation to deal with this new assault, but Amanda went on talking, in complete control not only of herself but, it seemed, of the proceedings in general. Even Nancy's high colour gradually subsided as Amanda continued. "Anyway, aren't we all rather wasting time? This isn't a debating society, I presume. Let's just say that like us all, Nancy is doing very well on the financial front, and that like all of us she finds the customers tedious. The only reason we're here this afternoon is because it was made pretty clear to us that we have to be. Either you knew, or else you've just found out from Judy, that Cleo had been in Japan before. I met her myself when she came here a few months ago. We all liked her, and we're all pretty shattered by the news. The people at the cabaret said we should cooperate with you, and I think we should. You too, Nancy love."

There was a brief silence, ended by a rumbling belch from Noguchi, who opened his eyes with an air of surprise, then closed them again. "Well, that's better out than in, I suppose," said Amanda brightly, and even Hélène and Judy managed wan smiles.

40

Kimura looked at his watch, which seemed to have stopped again in a perfectly maddening way. "Thank you, Miss Thorndike," he said. "I agree. I have no wish to keep you longer than I must, and there are one or two things I'd like to ask you all before Nakayama joins us."

He looked round again, and breathed in deeply. "First, I need to know whether she made a habit of, um, overnight work. After the cabaret closes."

Nancy grinned broadly for the first time, and her face was transformed. She wagged her head in mock censure. "*What* a suggestion, gee, that would be *immoral*!" she said in a cute-little-girl voice.

Amanda frowned. "Do shut your stupid trap, Nancy," she snapped. Then she turned to Kimura. "Be your age, sweety. We get a basic five thousand yen an evening, for five hours in the cabaret any time between six in the evening and two in the morning. Plus perhaps three to four thousand commission on drinks. If we skip out for an hour we can come back with another twenty-five thousand easy or of course wait till closing time and go case for probably more."

"Case?" Kimura was unfamiliar with the term.

"English usage, darling. Toothbrush, clean pair of knickers etcetera. All in a neat little carrying case. Cleo wasn't a popper-outer. She arrived latish, and generally went out with her case and an eager chap in tow. Of course, the cabaret management know *nothing* about anything like that." She winked at Kimura, and he nodded seriously.

"I see," he said. "I'm interested that she seemed to do so well. I've only her passport photograph to form a proper impression of what she looked like. She didn't look very pretty when I saw her body, I must say.

Kimura deliberately dropped the last few words one by one into an atmosphere grown suddenly chill. The French girl even suddenly clasped her own elbows as though physically cold.

Judy Cheng looked at Kimura, her small face grim.

"Cleo not so young maybe," she said. "Japanese men like very much, though. She speak Japanese good. She know what they like. Sometimes I go with her for specials."

This was one expression with which Kimura was quite familiar, and he nodded understandingly. "A hundred thousand for the two of you?" he enquired, and Judy nodded.

"A 'undred an' feefty when I went wiz 'er," Hélène put in unexpectedly, and Kimura began to feel that he was getting slightly out of his depth, though the blondeness of the French girl would certainly be highly marketable.

He cleared his throat. "Yes. Well. You say you were with her in Manila, Miss Cheng. Same sort of thing?"

Judy nodded. "Japanese mostly. They really like Cleo. Business men, tourist groups. Japanese men always go groups, you know?"

"Like dirty little boys," Nancy contributed, though her voice was more thoughtful than aggressive.

Kimura ignored her. "Right," he said briskly, looking at Amanda. "You told me to be my age. Now be yours, please. You know that girls on this game sometimes get hurt, even killed." Amanda's intelligent brown eyes held his, and she nodded slowly. "Well, it is quite possible that Cleo Ventura was killed by some pervert without any particular motive. But we have to check out everything we can. Think hard. Did she have any regular, particular man that you know of?"

The silence was almost palpable, and Kimura held it for several seconds. Everyone except Noguchi jumped when the doorbell range, and he was at the door and opening it before Kimura and the four girls looked round. "I am intruding," said a male voice in Japanese, and Noguchi shifted his bulk to one side and grunted. "Come in. You Nakayama?"

"Good Lord, Nackers did turn up!" Amanda's bell-like diction overrode Nakayama's muttered assent, and Kimura stood up as the newcomer entered the dreary little flat.

42

The centre of gravity now shifted completely to Noguchi, who looked the young man up and down. Nakayama was perhaps thirty or so, with a pasty, unhealthy-looking face. He was wearing a new, flashily cut light brown suit with a shirt and tie of chocolate colour, and had kicked off his shoes as he stepped up to the tatami.

"Listen," Noguchi growled without preliminaries. "This is Inspector Kimura. I'm Noguchi. Your boss told you about me." Nakayama nodded fearfully, a spike of hair sticking up from the crown of his head. "Few questions. This whole apartment block. Cabaret property, right? You're the protection for the girls here, right?" Noguchi jerked a thumb over his broad shoulder in the direction of the four at the table.

Now that the language was Japanese the whole tone became different. Even in what for Noguchi passed as polite conversation with Otani, he habitually used the plain male style of speech, and in talking to Nakayama he became crudely blunt. Nakayama's responses were hesitant, and those of an uneducated man. "Yes. I live downstairs. There are three of us. One of us is always here in case the hostesses have any . . . trouble."

Kimura cut in. "Bring men here, do they?"

Nakayama shook his head, very decisively. "No. Strict instructions from the manager. Not here."

Noguchi glanced at Kimura. "Ask her about him. The one with the brains."

Kimura was in no doubt who he meant, and spoke in English to Amanda. "This mans says that he or one of the two others is always available in the flat downstairs. Is that correct?"

"Mmm. I think of them as the Insurance Men. Nackers is an absolute pet."

"You mean Nakayama? Why do you refer to him as *Nakazu*?"

Kimura's accent, though extraordinarily good for a Japanese, brought out the vowel sounds in an oddly different

43

way from Amanda's, and she smiled. "Just our little joke. Because we think he probably hasn't got any . . . oh, never mind. Nakayama looks after us, runs errands and never asks for a bit on the side. We don't see so much of the one we call the Incredible Hulk. Hikino we call Fred. At least, Hélène and I do."

Noguchi had continued firing questions and orders at Nakayama while Kimura was talking to Amanda, and Kimura now returned to the Japanese wavelength. " . . . so get it straight, son. You won't be in trouble—any *particular* trouble—so long as we get what we want on the big one. These gaijin skirts are quite an investment for your boss. You can tell him from me that we'll blow his whole business apart unless we get those names. So long as we do, I don't mind looking the other way.

Noguchi caught Kimura's eye. "Finished?"

Kimura shook his head. "Not really, but we've got a few things to be going on with. Time to go, I think." He turned to the four round the table, then he took out his new lizard-skin wallet, from which he extracted one of his namecards. Standing over Amanda, he held it out to her. "Here's my telephone number. If I'm not there, ask for Asagumi or Sunao. They speak English. You haven't forgotten my question. I want an answer. Names of any special regular clients of Cleo Ventura. If you don't know names, describe the men to Nakayama here. He'll do the rest."

As Noguchi and Kimura left the flat the expression on Nakayama's face made Kimura reasonably confident that he would indeed do the rest.

Chapter V

"**T**HE FACT THAT THEY AGREED TO SET UP THE MEET-ing at all suggests to me that they're worried," said Otani reflectively, and he took a sip from the beaker of green tea he was nursing on one knee.

He, Kimura and Noguchi were in their usual conference configuration in Otani's big, old-fashioned office. Noguchi was lodged mountainously in one of the wooden-armed easy-chairs arranged with geometrical precision round the glass-topped coffee table on which stood the permanently empty cloisonné cigarette box. His cropped bruiser's head in repose against the lace antimacassar behind it, Noguchi was picking his teeth with a matchstick and staring unseeingly at the gloomy painting on the wall behind Kimura. It depicted a gothic sort of late afternoon in mountainous country, with a poorly executed animal which might have been a deer looking defensive in the foreground. Otani had occasionally been asked about it, by visitors, but was quite at a loss to account for its presence in his office.

Kimura was lounging gracefully on the sofa examining his nails and looking up from time to time to nod agreement with his superior, who occupied the other chair and addressed himself to the space above the table. Behind him was his big desk with the sheet of plate glass on top, and beyond that the window which looked out over the cranes and warehouses of Kobe Harbour. The square of dusty old carpet between them was rucked, and Otani pushed at it with the toe of his shoe as he spoke, smoothing it on the brown linoleum underneath.

Otani was the only one of the three in uniform, the neat dark blue of winter, though his blue-grey summer tunic was still on the coatstand in the corner on its bent wire hanger. "And now you tell me they've given you one or two names."

Kimura smoothed the silk sock over one of his ankles. "Well, descriptions mainly. They didn't mind admitting that she almost always took people to the hotel where she was killed." It was rather unfair, but Otani never minded leading Kimura on.

"The Fantasia. Typical of its kind, Chief. You'll remember I reported on it."

Otani nodded amiably. "So you did. Do they *really* have video recorders in most of those places nowadays? Any possibility that the killer may have left it on while he was there?" He stared at Kimura poker-faced, reflecting that "Murder in Slow Motion" would make an excellent title for a *krimi* novel of the kind he devoured at the weekends. He didn't recall the idea as having been used.

"More and more of the short-time hotel people are putting them in," said Kimura. "They're getting cheaper anyway, of course, and some places are even doing away with the five-hundred yen coin box charge." It occurred to Otani that it was as well that the Fantasia appeared to be one of them, or his ostentatiously casual demonstration of the machine to Hanae would have misfired. "They must be popular with the customers. Needless to say, we checked the tape in the recorder in the room, but it had been erased

46

since the last time it was used. People always erase them before they leave, of course.''

Noguchi suddenly snorted, and both the others looked at him enquiringly. ''Except when they take it away and put another blank in. Or bring a blank to record.'' Noguchi fell silent again.

''What would be the point of that, Ninja?'' Even as he asked, Otani realised that if Kimura rather than he had put the question it would have called forth all the withering contempt of which Noguchi was capable.

As it was, Noguchi merely grunted to himself for a moment, then responded more or less straightforwardly. ''Cheap way of making porno films. Porno cassettes, rather. Do it at home easy enough, but sex hotels already got the beds, mirrors, gadgets and so forth. Take a new tape with you, record it, make a few copies, hawk them around, twenty thousand each. Small-time stuff, but plenty doing it.'' It was, for Ninja, a longish exposition, and he closed his eyes in apparent exhaustion after it.

Kimura nodded complacently, as though he had made the point himself. ''Ninja's right, Chief,'' he conceded judiciously. ''Of course, if we *are* dealing with a real maniac, it's not inconceivable that he might have filmed himself in the act and taken the tape away to enjoy it at leisure . . .''

''Kimura,'' Otani said quietly, ''you have a revolting mind. What you say isn't beyond belief, though. The woman was battered to death very savagely, but the medical report didn't point to a psychopath. It was more the kind of blows you get when a normally controlled person goes berserk. I feel our man is unlikely to do it again, somehow.''

Otani swallowed the rest of his tea quickly, and put the beaker down. ''Well, let's get on. How far have you got with the leads the cabaret people gave you?''

Kimura sat up a little straighter and referred to a sheaf of papers he had on the sofa beside him. ''Well, first of

47

all, we've looked into the ownership of the Fantasia Hotel. Needless to say, there's a *yakuza* connection which links up eventually to the Love Box Cabaret, but it's a complicated one and we think it's unlikely to lead us anywhere particularly useful in this case.''

''Who's we?'' Otani had taken his glasses out of his tunic pocket in the expectation of looking at Kimura's papers, and was twirling them by one earpiece.

Kimura looked up. ''We? Why, my section. Actually, I put young Migishima on that particular line.''

Normally it was Otani who wandered happily down any sidetrack which opened up, but on this occasion it was Noguchi who diverted the discussion. ''He still going to marry that kid?'' he demanded abruptly. The question of Detective Constable Migishima's marriage had more than once claimed the attention of the most senior officers in the Hyogo force, for the good reason that he had asked Noguchi of all people to find him a suitable wife. It took a great deal to unnerve Noguchi, but he had bolted to Otani in a state approaching panic. Otani insisted that Noguchi should retain the nominal status of a go-between conferred on him by the young man, but had helped to identify a potential bride in the personable form of Woman Patrolman Junko Terauchi, of the Traffic Department. The introductory meeting had gone reasonably well, in spite of the fact that Noguchi had glowered throughout in acute discomfort and a new white shirt.

Otani smiled at his old friend. ''You ought to know better than the rest of us, Ninja. You're the go-between.''

Kimura stifled a giggle at the mental image of Ninja Noguchi officiating in that role at the actual wedding, and composed his face in an expression of gravity. ''I understand that they're getting along very well,'' he said. ''Migishima was mentioning that they're thinking of dates early in December, and I noticed some travel brochures about honeymoons in Hawaii on his desk.

Noguchi retreated into silent gloom, and Kimura and

Otani exchanged a look. Kimura cleared his throat. "So far as the Ventura woman's clients are concerned, it seems that the hostesses Ninja and I met at the English girl's flat gave us something of a false impression. We finally persuaded the cabaret people not to be stupid about withholding information, and were able to cross-check most of the statements the foreign women made. The Filipina was popular, and spoke really fluent Japanese—I gather all the others can make themselves understood, but no more. The Ventura woman made a lot of money. She would go with the occasional foreign tourists to one of the ordinary luxury hotels if he happened to be staying in one, but always used the Fantasia for her Japanese clients. She had to go somewhere like that when one of the others was hired for a three, of course. It seems she was particular, though. She would only go with well-dressed, professional sort of men. The *yakuza* boys were quite jealous—it seems she'd never give any of them a second look."

"What sort of professional men? Businessmen?"

Kimura shrugged his shoulders at Otani's question. "Well, it's usually businessmen who can afford to pay for that sort of extra," he said. "And doctors. They have plenty of money. It doesn't sound as if she'd be interested in the occasional farmer who sells a bit of land and goes on the town for a few days. We've checked out a credit bank manager who was one of her regulars. He was in Korea on business for the whole week when she was killed. At the moment we're working on descriptions of an architect and a politician. No names yet."

"If it turns out to be a member of the National Diet, let me know," said Otani casually, and Kimura laughed perfunctorily. "I'll do that," he promised.

A devil entered Otani's heart. "Particularly if it's a man called Yago," he added, watching Kimura's face. A strange expression came over it, but Otani realised that Kimura was looking not at him but at Noguchi. Turning his head,

49

Otani saw a look on Noguchi's battered face that was completely unfamiliar to him. Noguchi looked pale and ill.

"Ninja. Ninja! Are you alright?" Otani leaned forward, half rising from his seat, and slowly Noguchi seemed to recover himself.

"Sorry," he said shortly. "I'm alright. Just felt a bit off for a minute there."

Otani was concerned. He had no idea of, and never enquired about, Noguchi's domestic arrangements, but doubted if he had anyone very close who might look after him in sickness. The mere idea of Noguchi on sick leave seemed absurd. He hurriedly closed the conference, hustled Kimura away and quizzed Noguchi about his symptoms until, incredibly, Noguchi snapped at him and slouched out of the room, leaving Otani staring at a closed door.

After a while he stood up and crossed to the window, paying small attention when his clerk opened the door of the ante-room and brought in a small pile of incoming papers. It was not until he sighed and went back to his desk that Otani noticed the red special delivery endorsement on the topmost envelope, and recognised immediately the cypher of the National Police Agency in the corner. Communications from the Agency were by no means infrequent, and it was only with mild interest that Otani took up the paper-knife fashioned like a miniature samurai sword which had been given to him by a fellow Rotarian when he was accepted into the Kobe South Club.

The envelope had been sealed so closely that it was difficult to find a point of entry, but after wrestling with it for a while Otani managed to slit it open, only to find a second envelope inside, marked PERSONAL AND CONFIDENTIAL. Interest began to flicker in him, and he ripped the inner cover open carelessly and took out a flimsy sheet of paper headed with the words:

OFFICE OF THE SUPERINTENDENT-GENERAL

Like all official minutes, it was typed in the square phonetic script normally reserved for foreign words, which made for slower reading than the normal mixture of Chinese characters and cursive phonetics, and Otani went through it twice before folding the sheet carefully and tucking it away in his pocket.

He had been half expecting some sort of approach from the Director of the National Museum in Kyoto following his stupidly impulsive action in showing the netsuke to the Curator, but had certainly not supposed that they would go marching off to the NPA to lodge a formal complaint about him. Police disciplinary procedures were strictly codified, and perhaps for that very reason there was a good deal of reluctance to invoke them formally at any level, let alone that of a commander of a prefectural force. A telephone call from a member of the Prefectural Safety Commission suggesting a certain unease would have struck Otani as a fairly blunt instrument well within the reach of the Director of the Museum; yet here in his pocket was a letter, an actual *letter* bearing the seal of the Superintendent General, requiring Superintendent Otani, Tetsuo, to present himself at the headquarters of the National Police Agency at four in the afternoon of the following day for a preliminary enquiry into an allegation that he was in unauthorised possession of an item rightfully the property of the State under the stewardship of the Agency for Cultural Affairs.

Otani sat thinking for a long time, and even when he did turn to the other papers on his desk gave them only the most perfunctory attention. Then he looked at his watch. Four-twenty. Well, in twenty-four hours he would be in the thick of it. He pressed the buzzer on his telephone and ordered a travel warrant good for one official return journey to Tokyo, then took his bunch of keys from his pocket and opened the confidential filing cabinet in the corner behind his desk. There was very little in it: a number of circulars about security matters, some confidential notes on the principal figures in organised crime in the region, and a collection of exercise books of the kind used in schools,

51

in which Otani had written up some of the cases which he sometimes referred to as background material when he gave his occasional lectures at the regional police training college.

There was also a cash box, and Otani took this out and opened it with the smallest key on his ring. The netsuke had been safe enough there, in all conscience; probably safer than it would be in the museum. He lifted the little bundle out and extracted the carving from the paper handkerchiefs in which he had wrapped it, then closed the cashbox and put it back in the filing cabinet. The NPA people would certainly order him to hand it over, so it would have to go to Tokyo. It was an uncommon thing, certainly, and with the power to generate quite strong feelings, it seemed.

There was a tap on his outer door and it opened almost at once to admit Noguchi, who had obviously prepared a speech. Otani looked up and smiled. "You're looking more yourself, Ninja," he said, interrupting Noguchi's awkward apology for his earlier explosion. "I've just heard I shall have to go to Tokyo tomorrow morning, so I'm glad you came back." He stood up to cross to the easy-chairs, then noticed Noguchi looking at the netsuke. He quickly wrapped it up again and put it in his trouser pocket before moving over to where Noguchi was standing.

"What have you got there?" Noguchi demanded. "Netsuke, isn't it? Let me see it."

Otani raised an eyebrow. "Since when have you been interested in antiques, Ninja?" He kept his voice light and easy. "As a matter of fact it is."

"Where did you get it?"

Otani found himself beginning to resent the inquisition. He laughed briefly, without humour. "Ninja, you didn't come here to ask me about a piece of private property. Why are you so interested in a netsuke all of a sudden?"

"I want to know where you got it," Noguchi insisted mulishly, and Otani's temper snapped.

52

"Ninja. I'm sorry you're not feeling well. I'm making allowances for that. But I have no intention of discussing my private business with you. Now if you will excuse me, I have to clear up some papers before I leave. I'll look forward to seeing you again the day after tomorrow. Try to get some rest."

He nodded in curt dismissal and made as if to turn his back on Noguchi, but their eyes locked and they stood staring at each other for several seconds before Noguchi growled the single word "Sorry," turned, and left the room.

Chapter VI

"Oh, that's nice! I think I might come too," said Hanae happily when Otani told her that he had business in Tokyo on the following day. They were both dressed in blue and white cotton yukatas, and Otani felt a good deal better after his bath. Hanae seemed to have sensed that the day had left him out of sorts, and had come into the small bathroom of the old house in the foothills of Mount Rokko and begun to lather his back for him without being asked.

Then, when he was clean and rinsed and had stepped into the square tub and immersed himself in the steaming hot water up to the chin, she had stayed and chatted for a while, extracting only the information that Inspector Noguchi was unwell. Now they sat in the all-purpose downstairs room at the low table, bare legs dangling into the *kotatsu* pit underneath. The evenings were cold enough to justify putting the electric heater inside on to its lowest setting, but Hanae had not yet brought out the quilt that went over the table in winter and tucked snugly round their waists and hips to trap the heat below.

Otani fiddled with the rheostat switch at his side. "Father would never have approved of a gadget like this," he remarked. "He much preferred being half asphyxiated with charcoal fumes. I'd thought of taking an early Hikari train to get there in time for lunch with Kinoshita. I haven't seem him for years, and he suggested it when I rang to tell him I had a meeting at the Agency in the afternoon."

He had said nothing to Hanae about the reason for the summons to Tokyo. His visits there were fairly rare, not more than four or five times in a year, but occurred with sufficient regularity to occasion little comment. "You'd be very welcome to come along," he added hastily, seeing a look of disappointment flit over Hanae's face. "I'd half thought it might be sensible to stay overnight anyway. My meeting isn't till four, and might run on. Then you know what they're like. There's bound to be a crowd wanting to talk over a drink. You could have a good look round the shops and we could meet for dinner somewhere smart at about seven."

Hanae pursed her lips thoughtfully and picked up the *sake* flask from its lacquer holder, shook it and replaced it with the other one, which had been standing full in the pan of hot water at her side. "I don't really know," she said. "It's a lot of money to spend just for a few hours. If you've already arranged to meet Mr Kinoshita for lunch . . ."

Otani gave her bare foot a gentle kick. "Now you're making me feel guilty," he said. "I'm quite willing to put Kinoshita off. Then we can have the best part of the day together before I go to the Agency."

Even as he spoke, Otani knew that he would really prefer to face whatever lay in store for him alone, with time to himself both before and after, and realised also that Hanae knew him so well that she would almost certainly sense this.

She smiled, refilled his *sake* cup for him and shook her head. "No, it was just a silly idea. Next time we go to Tokyo together we'll make a proper holiday of it. You'll

55

enjoy seeing your old friends without worrying about keeping me waiting. Where will you stay? In the Agency?" Hanae was thinking of the small guest wing among the rambling buildings Otani had once pointed out to her several years before.

"No. I don't think they have those facilities in the new place. I'll go to one of the good business hotels like the Mitsui. Much better than sleeping on police premises, in any case." Otani felt relieved that Hanae had so quickly dropped the idea of going to Tokyo. It would have been difficult if not impossible to prevent her ferreting out the real reason for the journey during a three-and-a-half-hour train ride. Then it occurred to him that he was being unnecessarily close-mouthed about everything, and he smiled at her.

"Remember I told you about my visit to the museum in Kyoto?" Hanae nodded, and it seemed to Otani that she had a surprisingly high colour after no more than two or three of the tiny cups of warm *sake*.

Hanae had not in fact got round to mentioning her encounter with Kimura and their *tête-à-tête* over coffee on the same day. "Well, I thought I'd better take the netsuke to Tokyo and let the Investigation Bureau there follow it up."

She nodded vigorously. "I'm surprised that you didn't hand it over to the Museum there and then," she said, and Otani pulled a face.

"Look, Ha-chan," he said patiently. "I saw the photograph of the others, and I saw the expert's reaction. I agree that it seems virtually certain that the netsuke we found—"

"I found."

"—you found belongs to the same set. I should think it's almost certain that it will eventually go to the Museum. All the same, I have a perfectly reasonable police interest in finding out how it just happened to turn up hidden in a room in that sort of hotel: a room in which a woman had

56

been found murdered. Anyway, I just said I thought I'd better take it to Tokyo.''

"Did you bring it home with you, then?'' Otani nodded. "May I see it again before you take it away?''

Otani hauled himself up out of the *kotatsu* seat and straightened his yukata. "Very well. You *did* find it, as you just reminded me.''

By the time Otani returned from the upstairs room where they slept and where they kept their clothes, Hanae had cleared away the remains of their supper dishes, leaving only the *sake* flask and their two cups on the table. Otani noticed with satisfaction that the second flask was back in hot water, having obviously been refilled. "What on earth are you doing?'' he enquired, and Hanae, still rather flushed, produced a magnifying glass which she had been polishing on the hem of her yukata under the table. It was the one they both used from time to time for reading the unfamiliar Chinese characters which occasionally cropped up in letters, especially those from Hanae's sister, who taught history in a junior college and fancied herself as an intellectual.

"The perfect detective,'' he murmured as he settled himself again on his cushion and handed the crumpled paper-wrapped bundle to her. The light was bright in the small room, and Otani realised that it was the first time either of them had subjected the netsuke to close scrutiny. Hanae unwrapped it and peered at it intently, the expression on her face reminding Otani of their daughter Akiko as a little girl, frowning over a detail on one of the set of dolls in ancient court dress given to her by her stiff old grandfather on the first Girls' Day after her fourth birthday. Old Professor Otani had disapproved profoundly of his only son's choice of a profession, but unbent on that occasion to the extent of assuring the little girl gravely that the figure in the dress of the Captain of the Imperial Guard was "a kind of important policeman, like your father''.

Hanae studied the tiny carving from every angle while

57

Otani watched her quietly, sipping his *sake* and refilling his own cup from time to time. It seemed strange that such a funny little thing could be the focus of so much interest, and he found himself musing again over Noguchi's oddly peremptory questions about it. It was simply a small piece of ivory, carved in the likeness of a voluptuous woman in flowing robes. All at once a thought struck him, and he sat straight. "Let me see it for a moment," he said, picking up the magnifying glass.

Hanae handed the netsuke over and he brought the detail of the carving into focus. "What are you looking at?" Hanae enquired and he answered in a murmur, half to himself. "I was trying to see if there was any kind of hairline joint that might show up a secret compartment, but the neck is perfectly smooth and there's no joint at the base either. It just occurred to me that those old craftsmen were very proud of their workmanship. They were quite capable of hiding a jewel, for example." Otani was concentrating on the base as he spoke, and his voice trailed off.

"Have you found something?" Hanae's eyes were shining as Otani looked up.

"Nothing exciting, at least I don't think so. There's some very tiny writing of some kind on the fold of her robe there, but it isn't really hidden, and it looks as though it was done by the original carver."

"Let me see. My eyes are sharper than yours." It was true, and Otani handed the netsuke back to her. Hanae was very sensitive about the age difference between them, and often pretended not to notice when he felt old and tired.

"It's Greek," she announced confidently after peering through the glass at the area he pointed out.

Otani grinned, amused by her certainty. "You're guessing," he said. "Just because I told you it was probably a Greek goddess or *myuzu,* the man called them."

Hanae stared at him quite crossly. "I'm *not* guessing," she protested. "I recognise those letters. Greek is a funny mixture of ordinary roman letters like the ABC we all have to learn, and some different ones. Look, there's a kind of upside-down V.''

"All right Professor," said Otani, "what does it mean?" He grinned again, and this time Hanae kicked him, but he imprisoned her foot between his own and after an unconvincing struggle she left it there.

"I don't know," she said. "I'll copy it out on a piece of paper and see if I can find out, though." She resumed her inspection of the netsuke, turning it slowly under the glass. "The writing is *very* small," she said. "I wonder if there's any more?" Otani looked on reflectively. There could be little doubt that the inscription was part of the original carving, and that whatever it meant could have no present significance. The idea of a secret compartment was obviously ridiculous. He must be getting childish: foolishly childish, when on this occasion his taste for chasing hares had led him into an appointment the following day which at the very least would entail some disagreeable moments. The way to minimise them would be to turn the thing over to the Agency and let them get on with it. He would have to explain how he came by it, but with any luck the people in Tokyo would assume that it had been found during the original search of the murder room.

Almost absent-mindedly he caressed Hanae's warm foot with his own, and became conscious of a sudden tension as she spoke. "Darling," she said. They rarely used endearments, but this one served the dual purpose of indicating affection and seeking attention. Otani took the netsuke and the glass, and focused on the part of the figure Hanae was pointing at with her forefinger. "Look there. On the inside of the arm. I thought it was just a scratch, but it seems to be figures. Can you see?"

Otani held the carving up to catch the light at the right angle, and looked carefully at the mellow ivory. The patina was a rich brown in the folds and crevices, with scratch marks of obviously accidental origin here and there. He concentrated on the underside of the right arm. It was very difficult to see, but he thought he could make out lines of incision which went deep through the sheen and could possibly be figures or parts of them. The entire area involved was no more than a millimetre square. Otani put the carving down and rubbed his eyes. "Well, you may be right," he said heavily. "The marks certainly look as if they've been made deliberately, and whoever did it must have used a jeweller's tool or something."

"It's a message of some kind. I'm sure of it," said Hanae firmly. "You'll have to tell them in Tokyo. I expect they'll be able to photograph it somehow, and enlarge it. Whatever do you think it can be?"

"We can photograph it perfectly well in our own lab here," Otani said, picking up the glass and peering at the marks again. "I don't see why Tokyo should have all the fun . . . it makes me glad I didn't hand it over to the museum, anyway. Even if it turns out to be nothing." Furthermore, he realised as he sat back and looked at Hanae, he had been provided with what might prove to be an extremely useful justification for his actions.

"The problem is, I haven't time to organise it before I go in the morning, and I'd quite like to keep it to ourselves for a while."

Hanae looked at him in some surprise. "I thought the only reason you were going anyway was to take it," she said. "Can't you postpone your trip till later?"

"No," Otani said shortly, embarrassed at not having explained that he had been directed to go. "No. I must go now. I've fixed quite and important appointment. I'll take the netsuke along anyway. It's as safe in my pocket as anywhere, and I won't have time to lock it up again in my office. I might not necessarily hand it over, though."

"Leave it here," Hanae suggested. "I'll take care of it. It's foolish to carry it about when it's obviously important, or valuable. It's probably a very important clue."

"Where are you going to put it? Under the tatami mats?"

60

Otani smiled, knowing that this was where Hanae hid the rare letters he had written to her over the years.

"I shall not tell you," said Hanae with a haughty sniff. "It will be a lot safer with me than with you, though, you may be sure of that."

Otani shook his head. "I dare say you're right," he conceded. "All the same, I think I'll hang on to it. We'll fight about it in the morning. Tonight we'll put it on the floor beside us, where we can both keep an eye on it."

He swung his legs up and shuffled round the table on his knees until he was behind Hanae, then slipped his hands through the space under her yukata sleeves and cupped her warm breasts. She snuggled back against him contentedly. "Come, let's go to bed," he said. "People with business in Tokyo need to be sent off with affection. You're very observant, Ha-chan. Thank you for spotting the marks."

Chapter VII

OTANI HAD NOT EXPECTED TO BE IN A PARTICULARLY cheerful mood on arrival in Tokyo, but as he emerged from the gloomy brick tunnel which connected the terminus of the bullet trains with the original Tokyo Station he glanced up at the multi-storey banks and business offices of the Marunouchi district with approval. Tokyo was definitely improving, and Otani supposed there must be very few other capital cities in the world of which the same might be said.

It was just before eleven-thirty, and he had arranged to meet Kinoshita at noon at the little pork cutlet restaurant not far from the Metropolitan Police building where their senior people tended to go for lunch. There was practically time to walk, and Otani actually set out in the direction of the massive wall of the Imperial Palace grounds visible at the end of the broad avenue leading from the station before thinking better of it and stopping a taxi. The sky was as clear and blue as it had been when he left Kobe, but there was a nip in the air which would not reach there for another two or three weeks.

He sat back as the driver patiently negotiated the heavy

mid-morning traffic. He really must remember to compliment Kinoshita on the extraordinary achievement of the metropolitan force in taming the Tokyo taxis. The *kamikaze* drivers all seemed to have moved to the provinces in the last ten years or so. He had been irritated by what he thought of as Hanae's high-handedness in spiriting the netsuke away while he was shaving, but had come round to the view that it was probably just as well he had left it in her care. If they asked him outright if he had brought it with him he would be spared the necessity to decide whether or not to hand it over. It was something of a worry not to know exactly where Hanae had hidden the thing, but he had every intention of insisting on knowing when he telephoned her in the evening.

It took fifteen minutes for the taxi to follow the course of the inner moat round the palace grounds through Hibiya and towards the cluster of Ministry buildings around Kasumigaseki. There were a good many riot police on standby, their heavily armoured grey buses parked near most of the approaches to sensitive centres. Otani noticed that there were rarely more than two or three men in each of them, and usually only a single figure standing quietly outside each of the various gates, wearing the heavy blue, acid-proof coveralls, helmet with plastic visor, boots and gloves which Otani had himself donned from time to time in his earlier days. In the face of such grim accoutrements the fact that the men were armed with nothing more menacing than a long wooden baton came as something of an anti-climax and ordinary people bustled past them in the crisp sunshine without paying them the slightest attention.

It was obvious to Otani that it was a completely normal day in Tokyo and that no special security measures were in force. He was confirmed in his conclusion when he paid off his taxi at the Kasumigaseki business tower building just as a martial-looking truck cruised by with its loudspeaker blaring a wartime marching song. It was painted a dull khaki colour, and a large Japanese flag fluttered tautly from its standard at the back. The top was open, and two young men got up in battle fatigues stood at the front, grasping a grab-rail and gazing before them with stern dedication. Apart from the flag, the truck was festooned with slogans painted on white cloth. The Patriotic Party's current demand seemed to be for breaking relations with the Soviet Union to force them out of the occupied islands to the north of Hokkaido. The riot policeman standing on duty no more than two or three metres away from Otani gave the tableau no more than a perfunctory glance before resuming his stony impassivity.

"They come past most days around lunchtime," said a familiar voice behind Otani, and he spun round to see the familiar face of Superintendent Tadashi Kinoshita. "It's been a long time," they then said in delighted unison, bowing to each other for two or three seconds while the office workers beginning to stream out of the building eddied past them.

"You're looking very prosperous," Otani said as they finally straightened up and Kinoshita led the way inside and towards the basement where the various restaurants were located.

Kinoshita was the same age as Otani but was an altogether bigger man, and his large frame was indeed enclosed in a very smart suit. His shirt was dazzling in its whiteness and the tie was sober but elegant. "You make me feel quite the simple rustic in the big city."

Kinoshita did no more than smile in reply and set a cracking pace as he led Otani along the arcade towards a large sign bearing in impressionistic calligraphy the words "Number One Pork Cutlet". "I wanted to make sure we'd find seats," he explained as they went in to discover that they were just in time to do so. "I normally belong to what we call the French School and go for lunch at one o'clock. It's much quieter then. The twelve o'clock brigade seem to have the big appetites."

The little place was certainly at full tilt, even though it

was still a few minutes before twelve. The waitress who took their order was as civil and welcoming as all her sisters and brothers in the profession, but was obviously grateful for the businesslike way in which the two middle-aged men made up their minds. Otani declined the offer of a beer. "Must keep a clear head this afternoon," he explained.

Kinoshita nodded. "I was very pleased when you rang to let me know you were coming," he said. "The brainy boys at the Agency are a pretty tight-lipped lot, but I've heard one or two rumours."

The waitress brought their plates of food, and Otani raised an eyebrow as Kinoshita doused his deep-friend breaded cutlet with dark brown sauce from the bottle between them. "Rumours? What sort of rumours?" Otani had chosen the pork sauté, which came nestling on a bed of shredded raw cabbage with separate bowls of rice and of steaming bean-paste soup. The restaurant was now completely full, with two or three men waiting near the entrance for the first table to be vacated, and Kinoshita glanced round before replying. Satisfied that there appeared to be nobody he knew within earshot, he winked hugely at Otani.

"Promotion in the air?" he enquired happily. "When a prefectural commander comes to see the Big Man by appointment, what else are people to think? You've a lot of admirers in the Agency *and* in the Met, you know."

Otani never had much difficulty in keeping his face expressionless, and he attacked his lunch with apparent equanimity. "I rather doubt it somehow," he said after a while. "Anyway, what are your plans for later?"

Kinoshita looked at his watch. "Well," he said. "I expect you'll want to go to your hotel to check in before your meeting at . . . four, I think you said?"

Otani nodded. "Might as well." Like any other Japanese travelling on business, he was virtually devoid of luggage. Hanae had tucked a clean shirt and change of

65

underwear in his ordinary document case. There would of course be a freshly laundered cotton kimono in his hotel room, and a toothbrush and paste and throwaway set of shaving gear either in the bathroom or available for a couple of hundred yen at a dispenser in the corridor. "I suppose I ought to spruce myself up a bit, and I can leave my case there."

"Good. Well, a few of us would like to take you out for some drinks later on. To celebrate, you know. Why don't you come over to where the real policemen work at about five-thirty?"

Otani smiled wryly. "I don't know where you got this idea that I might have something to celebrate," he said in a mild voice. "Still, I shall probably be glad of a drink. Who's coming?"

"Oh, let's see. Teramoto and Urami from the old days, and Shimozawa you'll remember from Kobe. We'll probably pick up one or two from the Agency too."

It was really quite difficult to have a proper conversation in the restaurant, and before they parted Otani was able to do little more than discover that Kinoshita was keeping busy, that the politicking and rivalry between the senior officers of the metropolitan force and those serving in the National Police Agency was as lively as ever, and that his son had gone to America on a newspaper scholarship to study business management at a university Otani had never heard of but of which Kinoshita seemed to stand in some awe.

The hotel, tucked in behind the impressive shopping plazas of Akasaka, was conveniently near both the Agency and a whole range of bars and restaurants, and was as clean, impersonal and unpretentious as the so-called "business hotels" always seemed to be. Otani briefly wondered how they managed to keep the prices so moderate, but gave no further thought to his surroundings as, freshly bathed and fortified for the ordeal ahead of him, he left the hotel and descended into Akasaka Mitsuke subway station to take the Marunouchi Line back to Kasumigaseki, two stations away. It was Otani's first visit to the splendid new building which now housed the National Police Agency, and in spite of his preoccupations he was interested to see what it would be like. A far cry, no doubt, from the long low red-bricked building which he had grown to know quite well over the years and which now stood forlorn and deserted nearby.

Notwithstanding the riot police bus nearby, the two men on duty near the gate and the normal reception arrangements in the ground-floor entrance hall, Otani was not required to show his official identity card until he had taken the lift to the third floor and walked along a series of modernistic corridors to a special small lobby at the entrance to the suite of offices housing the Superintendent General of the National Police Agency and his most senior staff. Otani had not confided as much to Kinoshita, but his appointment was not in fact with the SG himself. It was with one of the Chief Superintendents of the third echelon at the Agency, under the SG and the Superintendent Supervisor.

The Agency was much more like a Ministry than a police headquarters, and its principal officials were served not by uniformed police officers but by civilian administrative and secretarial staff.

Behind a plain desk innocent of papers at the entrance to the Office of the Superintendent General sat a pretty girl in a neat red polka-dot blouse with a plain dark blue skirt of a brevity rather ahead of the current Kobe fashion. It reminded Otani of the miniskirts of the late sixties which had so shocked Hanae when their daughter Akiko took to them. He himself had thought them greatly preferable to the dirty jeans and sweatshirts of her student militant days, and he glanced with some satisfaction at the high-heeled shoes and slender legs of the SG's receptionist as she stood up to lead him into a reception room after politely asking to see his warrant card and checking the photograph on it with an intent frown. Tokyo legs, like Tokyo driving habits, seemed to be on the upgrade.

Otani had timed his arrival so as to be scrupulously punctual, but there was already quite a little reception committee waiting for him, standing in a cloud of cigarette smoke by the window. As he entered, the Chief Superintendent broke away and welcomed Otani with a perfunctory nod of the head. Otani had met him once or twice before, and though his grizzled, dried-out appearance reminded him of his own tedious assistant Inspector Sakamoto, he knew that Chief Superintendent Kawai had a reputation for astuteness which poor Sakamoto could never aspire to.

Kawai introduced the three other men in the room, by name and rank only. The trendily elegant one who might have been Kimura's twin brother was Superintendent Okada; the bald man with the rubbery comedian's face was Senior Superintendent Nitta, and the much younger fellow with a supercilious expression on his immature face was Assistant Inspector Morihara. Otani had never met Okada before, though he had heard about him as an up-and-coming younger man of his own rank tipped for a prefectural command before very much longer. He had over the years seen a good deal of Nitta, however, and his presence in the room came as a surprise. As the Chief bustled them all into the heavily brocaded armchairs round a shiny coffee table, cigarettes were handed round and the girl from outside came in with cups of green tea. Otani had time to wonder why the Senior Superintendent in charge of the Criminal Investigation Bureau had thought it worth diverting his attention from the probes going on into accusations of bribery and corruption in the highest political circles to spend even an hour over a tetchy complaint from the National Museum.

The young man Morihara seemed to have been brought in to keep some sort of record, since he positioned himself at a distance from the others and produced a notebook and ballpoint pen from his pocket. Kawai cleared his throat noisily and the desultory remarks being made comparing the weather in Tokyo with that of Kobe and commenting

68

on the exorbitant cost of tickets on the super-expresses of the New Trunk Line died away. Even then it took a little time to approach the real business of the meeting, for it was necessary first to apologise at some length to Otani for having intruded into his no doubt very busy schedule, and to thank him most sincerely for making the long journey to Tokyo.

Otani for his part then had to deny strenuously that he had been put to the slightest inconvenience, and counter by apologising for disrupting the Agency's arrangements at short notice and bothering senior colleagues with the affairs of a remote and insignificant provincial police force. The preliminary courtesies disposed of, Kawai cleared his throat again even more energetically, and there followed another short silence, broken only by Assistant Inspector Morihara, who sucked in his tea in a perfectly polite fashion but, in the absence of normal background noise, attracted general attention. He coloured slightly and put the cup down.

"Actually," Kawai continued with the inevitable cliché introducing a subject of some delicacy, "there has been a small problem about which we should like to have some discussion."

Otani nodded. "A formal compliant about me, I understand." A slight frisson evidenced itself among the men round the table at his bluntness, and the Chief nodded in his turn.

"That is so. A direct approach from the Cultural Affairs Agency to the Superintendent General. It is alleged that you have in your possession an object designated as a National Treasure and that you have declined to hand it over to the authorised representative of the Cultural Affairs Agency, namely the Director of the National Museum of Kyoto."

Morihara was scribbling busily, and Otani waited until he had finished before replying. Now that the thing was out into he open he felt both calm and confident. "The allegation is unfounded, sir. Both in substance and in de-

69

tail.'' Kawai said nothing, and merely rubbed the lobe of one ear. ''I have had no request from the Director of the Museum to hand over the object in question, nor is there any evidence that it has been designated as a National Treasure. The object in which the Museum is interested is in police custody as an item of evidence related to a criminal investigation, and will remain in such custody until the investigation is completed.''

''In police custody?'' Nitta's voice was fatly warm, like his whole manner. ''There is no reference to this, ah, netsuke, in the Hyogo headquarters inventory.'' The old devil must have been on the telephone that morning. Otani was discomfited. ''Don't you mean it's in your personal possession? This isn't really a formal disciplinary enquiry, Superintendent. I think we must ask you to be rather more forthcoming. I take it you're not accusing the Museum people of deliberate falsehood?''

Otani shook his head and sat back in his chair. ''No, sir, I am quite willing to explain the position informally. I wish the Director there had indeed approached me before the matter was taken up in this way. I have in my personal custody—in Kobe—an ivory netsuke which was found in a room in which a woman was murdered. In the process of establishing whether or not the object should indeed be regarded as material evidence I consulted not the Director but his assistant the Curator of the Kyoto Museum. I accept that there is a strong presumption that the netsuke is one of two missing from a set consisting originally of nine pieces. The remaining seven were, I understand, transferred to State ownership some years after the end of the Second World War, and these were designated as National Treasures. No such designation was made in respect of objects which at the time were not known to remain in existence: it could not be. Now, as is clear from my action in approaching the Museum authorities in the first place, I have made no attempt to conceal the fact that this netsuke has come to light. Nor will I put any difficulty in the way

70

of the preparation of a properly framed submission by the Cultural Affairs Agency that it should now be designated as a National Treasure. If such a submission is upheld, the netsuke will of course be handed over forthwith.''

Kawai permitted a tight smile to flit over his narrow mouth. ''You know quite well that those procedures would take months at the very least, Otani-san. Why do you insist on hanging on to it yourself? Properly handled, this discovery could bring great credit to the Hyogo force and to you personally. Imagine the headlines: Police Discover Lost Treasure. Not perhaps of world-shaking importance, but pleasant none the less in these disagreeable times. Instead of which you seem to be going out of your way to upset the Museum people.''

Otani shook his head. He realised that he no doubt looked as mulish as he felt. ''What I cannot understand is why the Museum people seem to be in such a great hurry,'' he said. ''They've done without the netsuke for thirty years or so, and had no reason to suppose they would ever have it: sooner or later they almost certainly will. In the meantime the more excitement it seems to generate the more convinced I am that it *must* be regarded as a piece of evidence, perhaps an important one.'' He picked up his own cup of tea, now stone cold, and looked up just in time to intercept a flicker of the eyes between Nitta and Okada.

Chief Superintendent Kawai sighed gently. ''You put us in a difficult position, Superintendent,'' he said. ''Technically, I cannot dispute your argument. Clearly you are not, as has been suggested, in breach of the Cultural Properties Protection Law. You seem in general to have acted within your powers of discretion, though I am bound to point out that they do not include the right to hold what is on any reckoning a valuable item without entering it on your official inventory. In your own interest the custody position must be regularised. If you insist that the netsuke remain in the hands of the police for the time being, I for my part must insist that it be transferred to the custody of this

71

Agency. Responsible officers of the Hyogo force will have access to it as and when you can justify it.''

He stood up and all the others followed suit. ''That is an order, Superintendent,'' he said sadly. ''It is unfortunate that you did not bring the object with you. Personal custody means exactly that. It does not mean leaving something in your safe at headquarters.'' Otani bowed in silence, wondering what Kawai might have said if he knew that the netsuke was not in the safe at headquarters, and that Otani had no idea exactly where it was at that moment. ''You will return to Kobe tomorrow? Good. An order for surrender will be sent to you. It will be up to you to ensure the safe delivery of the object to Senior Superintendent Nitta—the CIB will assume responsibility for custody until the legal position is clarified.''

The Chief Superintendent bowed curtly and led the way out of the room with Morihara in close attendance. Nitta lingered a moment as though about to speak, his mobile features comically contorted, then grinned broadly and himself left the room in silence.

Superintendent Okada remained. ''I'm glad to meet you at last,'' he said amiably.

''Hardly a jolly occasion,'' Otani replied. He was conscious of having won a minor victory, but at a considerable cost. Although Kawai couldn't nail him on a real charge, the irregularities of which he was obviously guilty were enough to justify a formal admonition; the first he had ever received. It all depended on how Kawai reacted to his unrepentant attitude. It had been impossible to judge from his manner whether he would in due course throw the book at him or forget the whole thing.

Okada smoothed his expensively barbered hair in a gesture strongly reminiscent of Kimura. ''Shimozawa over at the Met is a friend of mine,'' he said a little shyly. ''He told me some of your old friends are taking you out for a drink later. Um, he suggested I might come along. Would you mind?''

Otani looked him up and down, his spirits rising. It was quite obvious to him that Okada wanted to talk, and he could think of a number of things he wanted to ask him. "I'd be delighted," he said. "Shall we walk over to the Met building together?"

Chapter VIII

OTANI COULDN'T QUITE REMEMBER WHETHER THE BAR they were sitting in was the fourth or the fifth they had visited in the course of the evening, even though he established after a protracted and bleary study of his watch that it was still only a little after nine-thirty. The party had started out something like a dozen strong, laying down a solid basis of Korean-style barbecued beef with plenty of rice and a certain amount of beer at a noisy but cheerful place down a side street in Akasaka, and his former subordinate Shimozawa had kept everybody in fits of laughter with his descriptions of life at the British police college somewhere called Hendon. It seemed that he had just returned from training attachment there, and he was affecting a vaguely British style, mumbling comically with a pipe in his mouth.

The first bar they went to after the restaurant was something of a disappointment, and it had probably been a mistake to switch to Suntory whisky and water. Certainly they gained the impression that the bar mama thought it was rather early to start singing in wobbly sentimental voices, and they left after half and hour or so, at which point three of the men, whom Otani in any case remembered only dimly, reeled off in search of a Turkish bath. The diminished band had a much better time in the next bar, where Teramoto, who seemed to be able to speak English quite well, got into conversation with a visiting American business man and even acted as interpreter between him and the Japanese hostess to whom he wanted to describe his home town in Minnesota in some detail. They all looked at the photographs of his family which the American passed round, and sang a few more songs without attracting adverse comment.

It was after leaving there that they had lost Urami and Teramoto, who lived a long way from the centre, but Otani couldn't recall at what stage the others had peeled off, leaving him now with just Kinoshita and Okada in a small, quiet bar without hostesses. Apart from the young man tending the bar itself there was only the middle-aged mama-san, who seemed to be a pleasant, well-bred sort of woman. After greeting Kinoshita as an old and valued customer and receiving the information that Otani hailed from Kobe with apparently delighted astonishment and many expressions of goodwill, she had settled the three men comfortably at a corner table, brought them their drinks and a small dish of shredded dried squid to nibble on, then returned to sit with the only other customer, an elderly man she addressed as "sensei". From his appearance it was more likely that he was a professor than a doctor, but one couldn't be sure.

"He might even be a member of the Diet," said Okada when Otani asked his opinion. "They like to be called 'sensei' you know." He sat back and lit a cigarette, again reminding Otani of Kimura, though he was much less cocky and self-satisfied in his manner. Otani was uneasily aware that he had either drunk more than his two companions or held his liquor less well. Kinoshita was beaming amiably around, sipping from the glass he raised with a perfectly steady hand, and his broad face showed no signs of the dull flush that he knew suffused his own, having studied himself in the mirror in the tiny lavatory in the last bar. Indeed the hostess waiting for him outside to hand him a little damp hot towel for his hands had commented that he looked very well, and Otani assumed that the phrase had the same euphemistic meaning in Tokyo as it did in his own Kansai area of Japan.

"You must be tired," Okada said then. He had not been particularly loquacious on the way from the NPA to the Metropolitan Police Department headquarters to meet the others, responding rather unsatisfactorily to Otani's attempts to draw him out, and later had kept largely aloof from the boisterous conversation at the restaurant and in the various bars. Otani shook his head, wincing as he did so. His mouth felt dry and sour and his eyes were aching, and even while he was protesting gamely, he knew that he had passed the point of good humour and was beginning to slide down into depression.

"If I may say so, I thought the Chief was very impressed by your reaction this afternoon," Okada went on, his voice quite low. "He had to fetch you here, you know." Fuddled as he was, Otani nevertheless felt uneasy, and glanced at Kinoshita.

"It's all right," Kinoshita said. "I know about it. What Okada-san means is that the Agency has been under strong political pressure." Otani blinked and tried to straighten himself up.

"One particular 'sensei' has been pushing hard from the top," said Okada with a look across at the elderly man in deep conversation with the bar mama.

"Yago?"

Kinoshita looked surprised as Otani said the name, then nodded. "We may pretend to kid each other all the time," he said, "but some of us in the Met kept tight lines across to Okada-san here and a few of his colleagues at the Agency. Especially where the politicos are concerned. The Met has to supply the protection for Ministers and some of the other senior Dietmen, and we . . . let's say, keep an eye on a few more.''

Otani began to discern a glimmer of sense through the clouds of alcohol, and he looked from one to the other of his companions. ''Start again,'' he commanded in a reasonably businesslike voice, briskly enough at all events for the mama-san to look over at them enquiringly. Kinoshita grinned at her and pointed at their empty glasses.

As she waited at the bar for the young man there to prepare three fresh drinks, Okada spoke quitely. ''No,'' he said. ''*You* start. This particular lead begins with you. How did you ever come to hear of Yago in the first place? What do you think this netsuke thing was doing in the room where it was found?''

Their drinks were brought and Okada chewed thoughtfully on a piece of the squid while Otani summarised the conversation he had had with the Curator at the Museum in Kyoto. ''Well, that's how I learned of the Yago connection,'' he concluded. ''I can't begin to answer your second question, but there's another one that interests me more and more, and that is why it seems to worry so many people that I'm hanging on to the netsuke.'' It was so reassuring to be in the presence of senior colleagues he trusted that Otani was tempted to mention the writing Hanae had spotted, but something held him back.

Okada nodded reflectively. ''So far as I've been able to sort it out, the sequence of events here seems to have been that Yago first got at the Minister of Education. They belong to the same faction of the party, you know. Then the Minister contacted the Director General of the Agency for Cultural Affairs, which comes under the general authority of the Minister, and the next thing was an approach to the Superintendent of the NPA. I don't get the impression the complaint floated up from the Museum somehow, or it would have been dealt with at a much lower level. On the other hand, once Yago put it into the system from above, it would be simplicity itself for the Cultural Affairs Agency boss to find out that you'd been flashing the thing round the Museum.''

Otani nodded owlishly. He still felt extremely muzzy, and almost instinctively decided that it would be wiser on the whole to listen rather than talk. Kinoshita put his glass down and leaned forward. ''What interests us, and what I think you ought to ask yourself, is how Yago knew you had the thing in the first place,'' he said, and patted Otani on the thigh.

Otani blinked again. ''Why are you people keeping an eye on Yago? Because of his father?''

Kinoshita shook his head and drained his glass before replying. ''No. Yago's connections on the extreme right are hardly a police matter, and he doesn't make any particular secret of his views. No law against them. But you know as well as any of us that if you scratch a rightist you often find a gangster, and we're interested to find out where our friend gets his money. So are the tax people.''

As he finished speaking Kinoshita stood up and looked at his watch. ''Ten fifteen,'' he announced. ''What time are you planning to be off tomorrow?'' It was clearly the end of the evening, and Okada and Otani stood up as well. The floor seemed slightly unstable to Otani, but he thought that his brain seemed to be functioning reasonably well.

He managed a smile. ''Not too early, I think. I'll see when I wake up and what time I get to the station. I hope to get away by about ten or so.''

Okada looked him up and down as Kinoshita went over to the bar to settle their bill. ''I'd like to meet you for coffee before you leave,'' he said. ''I'll be in the lobby of your hotel from nine onwards. Don't hurry yourself.''

The three of them had a brief argument outside in the street. Kinoshita was for escorting Otani to the hotel, with perfunctory support from Okada. Otani had no need to fight very hard, though, and soon found himself sinking back into a taxi seat as the other two bowed extravagantly outside. The ride took rather more time that it should have done, mainly because of an extended jam near major excavation work for a new subway line which was going ahead under the glare of arc lights; but he was deposited at his hotel at a few minutes before eleven.

As he made his way, room-key in hand, towards the lifts Otani noticed a bank of pay-phones, including two of the yellow ones with the push-button dials which would take hundred-yen coins for long-distance calls. Examination of the loose change in his pocket produced four of them: quite enough for a goodnight word with Hanae. If she wanted to talk for longer she could always call him back in his room. He concluded that his first attempt produced a wrong number. Although their house was quite small, the nature of Otani's profession required that they should have two extensions to the main instrument in the downstairs entrance lobby; one in the room upstairs where they slept and one at the back of the house in the kitchen where it could be heard if he happened to be in the little garden trimming the miniature bonsai trees in their valuable old ceramic pots with the worn but delicately sharpened secateurs his father had used before him, and which fitted so justly in the hand. It was never necessary to wait for more than three or four rings for an answer, but to be on the safe side Otani counted to ten before trying again, this time concentrating with boozy deliberation on getting the sequence of numbers right.

Odd. He could have sworn he had made no mistake the second time, but again the ringing went on unanswered until at a count of fifteen he again hung up and retrieved the coins from the bottom of the box. He looked at his watch. Hanae would have been in bed perhaps half an hour, but in his absence was more likely to be watching television or leafing through one of the glossy women's magazines. It was much too late for her to be in the bath, and inconceivable that she had gone out. Unless . . . He put the money back in the coinbox and tapped out a different number. His daughter Akiko and her husband kept very late hours and might have tempted Hanae to spend the evening with them, in which case they would undoubtedly be keeping his infant grandson up far later than was good for him.

His son-in-law answered, and was mildly surprised when Otani identified himself, and calling from Tokyo at that. No, Hanae was not and had not been with them that evening. Was anything wrong? Otani controlled his mounting unease with difficulty, assuring Akira Shimizu that all was well, that to tell the truth he'd had a few drinks and had probably forgotten some plan or other Hanae must have told him about. After a little more desultory conversation and a final assurance from Otani that all was well, they said goodnight.

He had spent three of the hundred-yen coins, but thought he could easily have got hold of more from the night clerk at the desk, he decided to go up to his room, douse his head and face with cold water and take stock of the situation. It really was impossible for Otani to imagine where Hanae might have gone. There was of course no danger involved for a lone woman at night. He had often enough shaken his head in disbelief over the tales he heard about muggings and rapes in the streets of American and European cities. The only women who got into difficulties in Japan in public places were the occasional bar girl or whore at the centre of a drunken quarrel.

They had no car of their own. On official business Otani was driven about in his Toyota Police Special by the faithful Constable Tomita, and on private jaunts he and Hanae preferred the trains and taxis. Public transport shut down at around midnight till five in the morning, but taxis cruised the busier city streets throughout the night, doing good business with late-night revellers. These were invariably men, though, apart from women whose profession it was to keep them company.

Freshened up and by now coldly sober, Otani sat in his shirt sleeves on the edge of the bed in his small room and picked up the telephone. The hotel was evidently equipped with one of the new electronic memory banks to log long-distance calls, since there was no need for the services of an operator. This was a relief, and Otani dialled his home number again. It was eleven-thirty, and Hanae must surely be home by now, wherever she might have been. His spirits were already low, and he felt real fear developing as the empty ringing went on and on. She must be ill, lying just out of reach of the phone. Or electrocuted by some damned gadget or other. There had been enough cases of that sort of thing recently.

Otani looked at his watch for what must have been the twentieth time since returning to the hotel. There was no question of going to sleep. If it had been possible, he would have checked out and gone home immediately, but there were no night trains. He would have to wait till after six in the morning for a plane or a train, and in the meantime Hanae needed him. Of that he was quite convinced. He forced himself briefly to face the possibility that she might have taken a lover: after so many long years of marriage she might well have become bored with him. She was a very attractive woman still. Was it conceivable that she might at this very moment be writhing naked on a bed in a love hotel, sweating and moaning with pleasure at the caresses of another man? Feeling safe in the conviction that her husband would get much too drunk with his precious Tokyo friends to think about ringing her?

No. No. The thought was not only dismally mistrustful, but pointless. There was only one thing to do. Otani crossed to the alcove where he had hung his jacket, and took out the notebook in which he had written the contact telephone numbers of his senior officers. That for Noguchi was of an all-night snack bar in a district of Kobe into which Otani could not recall ever having ventured. Noguchi never talked about his private life, but on the few occasions over the years when Otani had rung the number and left a message, Noguchi had invariably called back within minutes.

This was a job for Kimura, though. There were six different numbers for him, five of them crossed out. Otani had never understood why Kimura liked to change his quarters so often, nor had he ever visited any of his various abodes. If the latest number he had proved to have been superseded recently, it would be necessary to call the duty officer at police headquarters, and that he was reluctant to do. It was with dull relief therefore that he heard Kimura's familiar voice at the other end of the line.

"Kimura-kun? Otani. Calling from Tokyo. I'm sorry to disturb you. I hope it's not too inconvenient. Look, I'm worried about my wife . . ." The conversation was brief but difficult, and after he put the phone down Otani lit a cigarette and lay back miserably. It would be an hour at the very least before he could possibly hope to hear from Kimura.

Chapter IX

IT WAS A LITTLE AFTER EIGHT-THIRTY IN THE EVENING, and Hanae was quite enjoying an evening to herself. In the old days it had been very different, with Otani liable for regular night duty and out till all hours even when theoretically on the day shift. Night duty was now a thing of the past, and it was comparatively rare for him to be away overnight on official business.

The November nights were becoming quite chilly, but it was warm and comfortable in the quiet downstairs room where she sat at the low table pink from her bath, at ease in a fresh cotton kimono, leafing through the December issue of a glossy women's magazine. Otani always used to complain at the publisher's habit of putting out editions dated weeks in advance, but Hanae argued that it wasn't only the women's magazines that were always ahead of themselves. Besides, it was pleasant to glance at the gorgeous photographs of year-end decorations for use both inside and outside the house, and to think about their own plans for the New Year. It wasn't too late to try again to push the notion of going somewhere warm, like Miyazaki or even Okinawa; but sad to think that Otani would never countenance a trip abroad. It made her feel awfully silly when the other ladies at the YWCA cookery class chatted airily about Honolulu and San Francisco, and even Paris and London.

She turned to the dressmaking pages and wondered again about the desirability of buying one of the new sewing machines that seemed to be able to do so many jobs. Now that they were really quite comfortably off it would be a perfectly manageable purchase, but then on the other hand she rarely went out socially and could afford to buy what clothes she needed for her modest wardrobe.

Her musings were interrupted by the sound of the telephone, and she scrambled up quickly and with mild surprise: it was on the early side for Otani to be ringing her. She had been visualising him out drinking somewhere with his friends, and smiling to herself at the thought that he would regret it the next morning. He liked his *sake* in the evening but was by no means a heavy drinker. It took a few seconds for her to adjust to the realisation that the awkward voice at the other end of the line was not that of her husband, but of Inspector Noguchi.

Hanae could not exactly say she *liked* Noguchi. He had visited the house two or three times over the years, and his clumsy attempts to be polite were rather touching, though she had always been rather afraid of his bull-like physical presence and air of barely restrained crudity. Of her husband's closest associates she greatly preferred Kimura, even though she knew quite well that he was the sort of man who simply couldn't help flirting with every woman he met. He had been perfectly charming to her over coffee, and if her heart had started to beat just a little faster when he took her arm . . . well, no need to be ashamed of that.

Now here was Noguchi-san, of all people, apologising for disturbing her, and muttering about the Superintendent having gone to Tokyo. Hanae was at a loss to imagine what Noguchi could possibly want, so naturally her assurances

84

of her delight at hearing from him were all the more elaborate and fulsome. A normal person would grasp at once that she was distinctly put out, but Noguchi made no attempt to mollify her in any of the accepted forms of words. On the contrary, he went on almost at once to talk about the netsuke. Although she was not in any real sense acquainted with Noguchi, his character was one of Otani's favourite topics of conversation, and Hanae felt as though she knew him well. This was the first time she had spoken to him on the phone, but she became convinced as he went on that he was ill at ease. Nevertheless, it was clear that he had to be headed off.

"Netsuke? I'm very sorry, but is this some kind of police business? I think it would be better if you were to speak to my husband about it . . . if it's urgent I could leave a message for him at his hotel . . . I expect he'll be there by ten o'clock or so." Again the receiver crackled in her ear as the gruff voice blundered on. Hanae listened quietly and attentively. It seemed that the inspector knew quite a lot about the netsuke and had been discussing it with Otani the previous day. Hanae found herself resenting this: it was in a sense *her* netsuke, after all. Noguchi was now asking bluntly whether Otani had taken the netsuke to Tokyo with him, and from the way he referred to it there could be no doubt that he had seen it.

She spoke with a rare tartness of manner. "Noguchi-san, I really must explain that police matters are no concern of mine. I cannot imagine why you seem to suppose that my husband has discussed this . . . netsuke with me or that I understand what you are talking about. My husband will be back in Kobe tomorrow and I suggest that you talk to him then. As I say, if it is urgent I can tell you where he is staying tonight."

There was a very long pause, which bothered Hanae rather more than Noguchi's actual words had done. Then with the briefest and most curt of farewells, Noguchi rang off and Hanae returned to the table troubled by the whole conversation. Noguchi had after all referred to the netsuke as an important piece of evidence, so he must know a good deal of the background. It was his edgy insistence that the netsuke must not, as he put it, be left lying around that bothered her. It was strange that Noguchi should think for a moment that Otani might have left the netsuke at the house, when right up to the last moment he had fully intended to take it to Tokyo.

She turned again to the two pieces of paper on the table beside her magazine. One of them bore the single Greek word ΚΛΣΙΟ, copied by Hanae with scrupulous care from the book they had very kindly fetched for her from the basement of the Prefectural Library earlier that day. Hanae was no great reader, and it took some time for her to explain to the girl at the desk what she wanted. Even then the girl shook her head worriedly, and it was not till she led Hanae through to a thin young man at another desk inside the library that she made any headway in her quest for a book about the Greek Muses. At least the young man had heard of them, and found one or two picture books full of broken columns and statues which for the most part lacked arms, noses and not infrequently heads. Then he disappeared and came back after a while with an armful of travel books, explaining that they had a great many by Japanese professors who described their visits to Europe from a scholarly point of view.

The young librarian became quite enthused, and poured through the indexes while Hanae turned pages in a bewildered way. The books seemed to go into a good deal of detail about travel and hotel arrangements, but she became momentarily interested in an account of a meal one author had eaten in a place called *Asenzu*, which, the young man reminded her, was the capital of Greece. The vine leaves sounded as though they might be almost as nice as chrysanthemum leaves, but she shuddered at the thought of roast baby lamb and closed the book just as the librarian uttered a small cry of triumph and pointed to a list of Greek characters in the book he was holding open.

The erudite author had obligingly transliterated the names into Japanese phonetic script, and Hanae now knew that the inscription on the netsuke which had been burning a hole in her handbag throughout her visit to the library was pronounced *Kureio*, and that the lady of that name was the *myuzu* or goddess of history. On her second sheet of paper Hanae had written, in phonetic Japanese script only, the names of all nine goddesses, mainly because the librarian had seemed to expect it of her. Arriving home at Rokko it had been a relief to be able to put the netsuke into the place of concealment in which it would remain until it was needed, and which Otani could not possibly guess but which he would infallibly find. *Kureio*. A strange but not unpleasant-sounding name. Certainly among the more euphonious of the nine; though Hanae quite liked the sound of *Merupomini*, which for some reason made her think briefly again of Hawaii.

Hanae had more or less regained her composure after Noguchi's telephone call and was beginning to allow herself to hope that before long she would receive the one she was looking forward to, when all at once she was startled by the sound of the doorbell, and without thinking looked at the clock. Ten past nine. An extraordinary time for a caller, unless it were the postman making a special delivery. Even so, Hanae would normally have opened the sliding front door without the slightest hesitation. This time a residual unease resulting from Noguchi's call made her feel nervous. Surely the inspector hadn't taken it into his head to come to the house? What on earth should she do if he had?

The inner porch where people took off their shoes before stepping into the house was in darkness, and before turning on the light Hanae peered at the door, which was of heavy frosted glass panels in a frame of wooden uprights, each panel about three inches wide. The figure of her caller was dimly visible, and the shadow was certainly not that of the bulky form of Inspector Noguchi. It was indeed quite obviously that of a woman, but even so Hanae spoke rather timidly. *"Moshi-moshi?"* It didn't exactly mean "Who's there?" but at least constituted a reasonably polite enquiry.

The reply was similarly tentative, and the voice that of a well-educated woman. "Is this the Otani residence? Mrs Otani perhaps? I am so sorry to trouble you at such a late hour." Hanae admitted through the closed door that she was Mrs Otani and waited for further word.

When it came it was greatly reassuring, and Hanae opened the door while the woman was still speaking. " . . . so of course as a social worker I find it difficult to make these calls earlier in the day, but the neighbourhood association head said I would be sure to find generous people in this area who would understand what we are trying to do for the welfare of the handicapped Koreans in Kobe . . ."

She looked as if she was about Hanae's own age, and her voice was warm and persuasive. She was wearing a good but not especially fashionable coat, and was carrying an open, ruled notebook in which was written a list of what looked like names, descriptions and addresses; amounts of money were entered at the side of each. Hanae smiled with no more than correct courtesy, and nodded as the woman went on earnestly to detail the activities of the Society for Helping Handicapped Koreans. It was all predictable and fairly typical, even the conclusion that the Society felt that an appropriate contribution from the Otani household would be two thousand yen.

Hanae nodded and excused herself to go and fetch her purse from the kitchen, leaving the woman standing in the entrance. They had been asked for and had paid more for the Indochinese boat people, less for the victims of the Minamata disease. There were two or three campaigns of the sort most years, and Hanae rummaged philosophically in her purse for a couple of thousand-yen notes, reflecting as she did so that it always seemed to be busy people, like social workers for instance, who found time to devote to worthy causes. Though the lady at the door had at least managed to fit in a visit to an expensive beauty shop judging by the elegance of her hair-do.

Hanae found the two thousand yen and had just opened the kitchen drawer to find some kind of envelope to put it in—she had a well-bred aversion to the idea of handing over what her mother had always called "naked money" except to tradesmen—when it happened. The arms snaking round her were curiously gentle at first, and for one disbelieving moment Hanae froze with the thought that the woman was making a sexual approach to her. Then she began to struggle wildly, but the collector for the Society for Helping Handicapped Koreans was too strong for her and though Hanae scrabbled furiously at the pad clamped over her nose and mouth the pressure was maintained. In quite a short time Hanae was crumpled unconscious on the floor. The woman bent down and straightened out her kimono, decorously covering a thigh which had become exposed, then went to the front door.

Chapter X

KIMURA STOOD GRIMLY NEAR THE GLASS DOOR THROUGH which the Tokyo passengers were beginning to emerge. It was a quarter to eight in the morning at Itami Airport, and he was wearing his plainest, most unobstrusive suit. Even the weather was sombre, with dull grey clouds piled up over the hills to the north, and there had been a spatter of rain as he had left headquarters an hour earlier in Otani's official car with Tomita at the wheel, as soon as the curt telephone message was received to confirm that he would be on the first plane of the day to Osaka.

Kimura himself was tired, though a night without sleep from time to time usually bothered him little. It had been annoying to have to get out of bed the previous night and leave Trudi from the German Consulate with her golden hair spread over the pillow in his quiet little bedroom, but it would have been worse if Otani had rung half and hour earlier. Besides, if previous experience was anything to go by it would have been difficult to the point of impossibility to wake her for a second session before breakfast time. She hadn't even moved when he went back to shave and dress

90

properly at about five, but then he had often enough had to leave her to make her own way out in the morning.

It had seemed an absurd errand as he climbed into the taxi and told the driver to take him to the Otani house at Rokko, and during the fifteen-minute drive from his own flat at Ashiya he wondered what on earth he would say to a drowsy Mrs Otani roused from her bed well after midnight. As soon as he opened the tall wooden gate, approached the front door and tried it gently he realised that something was amiss, though, for it slid open to his touch. This would have been normal enough by day, but not late at night, especially with the head of the household away.

Calling Otani at a hotel in Tokyo from his own house in Rokko had seemed as strange as it was painful, though apart from a sharp intake of breath Otani had given no audible reaction to the news that there was no sign of Hanae, and that though the house was in no great disorder it was Kimura's opinion that it had been gone over pretty systematically. Kimura's own thoughts were in turmoil, and he could not begin to imagine what must be passing through the mind of the haggard man who now came through the doors of the arrivals lobby at the airport.

Kimura bowed in silence, then fell in at Otani's side. Otani himself did not break his step as his eyes met Kimura's, and he said nothing when Kimura gestured in the direction of the car. Tomita sprang out and held the door open and Otani sank heavily into the back seat, making no attempt to move over. After a moment's hesitation, Kimura opened the front passenger door and climbed in beside Tomita, who looked at him with astonishment, then waited expectantly for orders, his eye on the rear-view mirror. They sat like that for several awkward seconds, until Kimura broke the heavy silence. "To Rokko, sir?" It was barely perceptible, but looked like a nod from Otani, and Kimura whispered "Rokko" to Tomita.

At that early hour the traffic was still fairly light, and they made good time to the house, which now had a patrolman standing on duty outside. Only Kimura acknowledged his smart salute, while Otani swept into the house, kicking off his shoes as he went in. Then he uttered the first words he had spoken since arriving at the airport.

"Wait down here."

Kimura was used to be barked at, teased, and on occasion magisterially rebuked by Otani, and the bluntness of the instruction was not in itself out of the ordinary. What troubled Kimura was the note of utter misery in Otani's voice.

After perhaps fifteen minutes Otani came slowly down the stairs again and once more disappeared, this time in the direction of the kitchen and bathroom. Eventually he emerged from the living room and looked at Kimura dully. "Come in here," he muttered in the same dead voice, and Kimura hurriedly took his own shoes off and stepped up on to the tatami mats. Otani was not so much sitting as crumpled, one shoulder against the subdued brown of the rough plaster wall, and Kimura remained standing until Otani listlessly waved him down.

"You were right," he said at last. "It's been turned over, but carefully."

"Is anything missing?"

Kimura would gladly have bitten off his own tongue when he saw the furious blaze in Otani's eyes. *"My wife's missing, damn you!"* he bellowed, sitting up straight and visibly quivering. Kimura hung his head, and after a moment Otani apologised. "Sorry, Kimura. A bit on edge. Tell me again. From the time you got here."

He listened attentively enough to Kimura's report, as he had done so many times before, but Kimura found his own sentences trailing off indecisively as he looked at the pain and anxiety in the face of the man staring at him in silence. There was little enough for him to say, and it took only a few minutes for him to explain what few steps he had been able to take to locate anyone who might have seen something untoward at the house the previous evening. It was reasonable to tell his chief that he had already checked the hospitals and clinics of the area to see if any woman answering to Mrs Otani's description had been admitted as an accident victim, but the expression on Otani's face was enough to rule out the possibility of asking him whether he wanted a full-scale missing person investigation launched, with all the attendant publicity.

When Kimura finished, Otani closed his eyes and rubbed them for a while, then looked at him again. "Yesterday. When I was in Tokyo. There was a call from Senior Superintendent Nitta of the NPA. Who took it?" The question puzzled Kimura, and with something of an effort he turned his mind to the events of the working day, which now seemed to have receded into the remote past.

"Yes, that's right. There was a call, but I thought it was from someone in the Criminal Investigation Bureau, not Nitta himself. I was talking to Ninja in my room at the time. I was duty officer. The fellow at the Agency wanted to have details of the inventory of articles we're holding in connection with the Ventura murder. I read the list over to him, though I couldn't see what concern it was of theirs at this stage: after all, they didn't ask to take over the investigation from us when we made the initial report."

"Did they ask about any particular items?"

Kimura breathed in reflectively, then shook his head. "No," he said slowly. "Not when I was talking to them, anyway. We'd pretty well finished the conversation, and I was going to ring off, then Ninja said he wanted a word with them and I gave him the phone. Then I was called away urgently and left him to it. He didn't say anything afterwards . . . we could ask him, if it's important."

Otani shook his head, then heaved himself laboriously to his feet. "We'll go to the office," he said very quietly, and neither man spoke again as they put on their shoes and went out, Otani locking the door behind him with a key from the ring he produced from his pocket. Although this time Otani beckoned Kimura to share the back seat of the car with him, the silence was maintained throughout the drive into Kobe and as they walked into the main entrance of Hyogo Prefectural Police Headquarters. Eventually Otani spoke as he headed for the staircase and his office. "I'll send for you later," was all he said.

Otani sat slumped in his big chair for a long time, thinking the unthinkable. Noguchi. It had to be Noguchi. It *couldn't* be Noguchi, yet it *must* be Noguchi. He looked again at the open file before him on the desk. It was the first time to his recollection that he had ever bothered to study the confidential personal file of Inspector Noguchi. Indeed Noguchi always seemed to be above such things as pay and conditions and promotions. He seemed to have his existence solely in the shadowy context in which he had worked for so many years, like the spies and assassins who were known as *ninja* employed by the feudal barons of former centuries and after whom Noguchi was flatteringly nicknamed. It was strange to read the cold objectivity of the brief biography attached to the inside cover of a file. Strange to know that he had been born a countryman, in Aomori Prefecture away to the north, where the apples came from; that he had attended the local school and even managed to get through middle school before being sucked into the war.

Otani had always taken it for granted that, as a man several years older than himself, Noguchi must have served in the armed forces, but Otani was the unconventional one in being quite willing to chat about his Navy days. Noguchi was like most men of his generation in seeming to blot the war years from his recollections or at all events his conversation. Now it was confirmed in faded blue ink on the form: "Served in Imperial Army between the sixteenth and twentieth years of the Showa Era." Who would have thought the old Emperor would still be on the throne forty years later? Military Police: security detachment, Imperial Staff Headquarters, Tokyo; then at General Headquarters

Hong Kong and finally in the Philippines. He must have been good . . . comparatively few non-graduates were commissioned, but Noguchi had been a provost lieutenant when the Americans captured him. Then after repatriation he had been one of the hand-picked few, like Otani himself, to be enlisted into the fledgling civilian police reserve in the very early days of the American occupation of Japan.

This man, this old friend and intimate associate for well over a decade, was the only person apart from Hanae and the Curator at the Museum who had seen the netsuke in his possession. It was Noguchi who had reacted so sharply to the sight of it; and earlier to the mention of the name of Yago. It was Noguchi who knew that he would be away overnight, leaving Hanae alone in the house, and might have guessed that he could have decided to leave the netsuke there. Everywhere he twisted his mind, Otani found Noguchi.

He had never been so naïve as to suppose that senior police officers were immune to corruption, and indeed had a shrewd idea which of the members of his own force lined their pockets. When lecturing at the regional training college on the subject of ethics he was often hard put to it to maintain his famous poker face when expanding on the sections of the handbook which urged young policemen to avoid premarital or extramarital sexual relations with and the acceptance of even modest gifts from grateful members of the public. Otani was much too well aware of the toughness of the social web of Japan to imagine that policemen could free themselves from its clinging demands and compensatory benefits.

Noguchi's work was almost wholly in relation to organised crime at every level, and he was on terms of close acquaintance with far more gangsters than with law-abiding citizens. His ostensible concern was the control of the traffic in drugs, but that was just one aspect of the totality of commercialised vice and exploitation of vulnerability, and there was little Noguchi didn't know about the other interests of the gangs, including the grey area where their activities shaded almost imperceptibly into the legitimate.

Otani tried to numb the pain of his anxiety over Hanae's disappearance by forcing himself to think back over the years of Noguchi's achievements as head of the Drugs Section of the Hyogo force. Apart from negative evidence, like the fact that they had good reason to be proud of their statistical record in comparison with other prefectures of the same general characteristics, there had been some notable coups, including the round up of a good many gangsters. It had indeed been one of these who had in court first bitterly likened Noguchi's unexpected apparition on the scene of a huge payoff meeting to that of a *ninja*, and the name had stuck. True, he had never netted a really big one, but for that matter no police officer in the country ever had or would. The ultimate bosses of the principal gangs to which lesser fry formally affiliated themselves took good care to keep their personal activities on a scrupulously legal basis, with a series of cut-outs at various levels which effectively ruled out any possibility of making a charge stick. Unfortunately Japan's penal code was virtually silent on the subject of conspiracy; except to cause a riot, which was the last thing the *yakuza* chieftains wanted to do.

On the contrary, they were the most conservative of men, with a vested interest in social tranquility and economic prosperity, from which they could cream off their vast profits. They often played at politics, almost always on the lunatic fringe of the right wing, inventing parties with grandiose names like the Great Imperial Patriotic League or the Love of Country Anti-Soviet Alliance, and sponsoring reunions of ex-servicemen at which the old songs were sung and fervent speeches were made. It was no secret that a good deal of their money found its way into the right-hand side of the political mainstream, too, and this was possibly why Otani's colleagues in Tokyo were taking an interest which scarcely seemed to be warranted by Hanae's discovery of an ivory carving whose value to collectors could not possibly be more than a few million yen at most, even if it did seem likely to end up as a designated National Treasure.

Otani stood up wearily and went to the window. There must be a gusty wind outside, because raindrops were streaked across the glass obliquely. The sky was leaden, and he shivered, though it was warm enough in the room. Could Noguchi conceivably be behind the killing of the Filipino woman? Why, in the name of all the gods? He never seemed to take much interest in money, and certainly never spent any on himself, except for food and drink; but that didn't cost much in the scruffy bars and eating-houses he preferred. Blackmail? Impossible to imagine Noguchi as being vulnerable. Yet there must be a connection between the Filipino woman, the netsuke and the man Yago; and that connection somehow involved Noguchi.

Otani suddenly realised that he had a burning cigarette in his hand, but had no recollection of lighting it. He crossed to his desk and stubbed it out, startled to see at least eight or nine more stubs in the ashtray which had certainly been empty when he entered the office—he looked at his watch—not more than an hour and a half earlier. There was a gentle tap at the door, which he ignored. Then another, and the handle turned. With the door half open, Kimura peered cautiously round it. Otani said nothing, and he entered, leaving the door open.

"Sir. Sir, you ought to get some rest." It was rare for Kimura to be so quietly courteous. What he said was true. There was a sick dullness in Otani's head which he knew with part of his mind was due in no small measure to simple exhaustion. Yet sleep was out of the question. Hanae had quite certainly been abducted, and his agony of mind over what might be happening to her made it quite impossible to consider the question why. Even during his distraught search of the house it had become clear to Otani that whoever had been through the place must have been looking for the netsuke, and for all he knew they had found it. Beyond that his mind spun crazily, its gears stripped.

"I can't go back to Rokko, you do see that, Kimura?" Otani spoke in a wondering, almost reflective way, almost as though he were intellectually interested in what he was saying. "Not with my wife missing."

Kimura thought quickly. "Let me take you to your daughter's flat," he said. "You must have somebody to take care of you." Otani started to shake his head, then stopped as a black wave of physical pain surged through his neck and skull. He weaved slightly, and steadied himself with hand against his desk as Kimura moved towards him quickly in concern.

"I don't want to be a nuisance to them," Otani muttered vaguely as Kimura led him unresistingly out of the office and down the stairs towards his car.

Chapter XI

For a moment when she came to, Hanae thought she was in their own bed on the tatami-matted floor of the upstairs room at Rokko. The bedding was clean and fresh, and her cotton kimono was straight and uncrumpled round her body in the way Otani always marvelled at. It was when she moved and became aware of a nauseating metallic taste at the back of her throat that the recollection of the woman's arms pinning her and the sweet sickening smell of the pad over her nose and mouth flooded back, and it was all Hanae could do to prevent herself from vomiting there and then.

The room in which she found herself was in darkness, and she forced herself to lie very still until she was able to discern the line of a window-frame and what might be a sliding *fusuma* screen door on the opposite side of the room. Cautiously Hanae felt about on the tatami mats on either side of her head, roughly where an electric lamp would normally be placed, but there was nothing within reach. She realised with part of her consciousness that dark terror was waiting, as it were, ready to overcome her all in good time. The immediate imperative, though, was to yield to the horrible lurchings of her stomach and throat.

Retching horribly, Hanae crawled toward the sliding door and managed to get her fingers into the crack. It yielded a little, and she was able to inch it open. It was just as dark outside, but Hanae could see enough to realise that she was in a small apartment, small enough for her to be able to get to the bathroom in time. The relief when she just made it and flushed the sour mess away was enough to make the terror back off for a while, as she pulled herself unsteadily to her feet and found the light switch. The lavatory was Japanese-style, small and tiled in speckled blue and yellow like an exotically-coloured bird's egg. It was clean, and there was paper, with which Hanae thankfully wiped her mouth before moving to the wash-hand basin in the adjoining bathroom and rinsing away the remaining foulness.

She still felt weak and sick, but her body was becoming quiescent, and it was then that the fear pounced and possessed her fully. Gripping the edge of the basin Hanae stared at her reflection in the mirror, seeing herself as a frightened, lonely old woman, years in the future. Her normally tranquil, well-nourished face looked gaunt and pallid, and wisps of hair clung damply to her forehead and cheeks. There were dark smudges under her eyes, and her mouth was tight and drawn.

Then, mercifully, the tears came and she allowed herself to slide to the floor, sobbing out her bewilderment for what seemed a long time. As she did so a flicker of strength seemed to bud and grown in her, and the blind longing to hide in her husband's arms began to lose its obsessive power. To Hanae's own weary surprise, an image from her girlhood rose up in her mind. She was eight years old, kneeling immobile in the presence of her father in the stern austerity of the reception room of the family house in wartime Tokyo. Her legs ached, but having been schooled from the age of four to remain utterly still when in the formal presence of any male adult, above all the head of the household, it never occurred to her to move as the tension built up. Although the memory of the occasion became vivid in her mind, and she could see the small girl she had been almost objectively, and recall the detail of the dull mauve and black stripes of her threadbare kimono, she could not at all remember whether or not her mother had been in the room as the solemn strains of the national anthem swelled and faded in the crackle of the monumental wireless set, in front of which had been placed a black-swathed photograph of her elder brother, stern in his Army uniform.

On entering the room she had been puzzled to see in front of the photograph a flat lacquer dish on which had been placed two small hard rice-cakes, one on top of the other, and a dried-up shrivelled tangerine. To either side were tiny brass bowls from which wisps of smoke from incense spiralled up in the hot, still air. She had been told only that the voice of the Emperor would soon be heard for the first time ever by his common subjects like themselves, and supposed that it would sound something like the splendid surge of the instrument on one of the scratched gramophone records which belonged to her brother, and which her mother told her was called an organ. The wireless set crackled, and a man spoke, then another. She could understand only the odd word here and there in what seemed to be very strange old-fashioned language, and waited patiently for the Emperor, whose sacred grandfather's Rescript on Education was read aloud to her and all the other children at school every morning in assembly before they all bowed low in the direction of the Imperial Palace.

The national anthem was played again, and little Hanae bowed humbly in imitation of her father. Now surely His Majesty's voice would be heard. Bewildered, the child watched as her father wearily rose to his feet and beckoned to her. Crumpled on the bathroom floor, Hanae heard herself asking when the Emperor would speak, and felt again the hot tears which had stained her face as her father explained gently that His Majesty had spoken, that the war was over, and that there would be no more bombs, no more of the terrifying fires which had come so near to their house on many occasions, and that the spirit of Elder Brother would be at peace now.

The recollection of that day triggered off others, but it was probably only a few minutes later that Hanae again pulled herself upright and this time systematically washed herself. There was soap, there was a small towel, and she even found a comb in the small cabinet on the wall which otherwise contained nothing but a half-empty bottle of expensive imported shampoo. At least, she reflected sombrely, she could be frightened with clean hair; though a toothbrush and paste would have been more welcome at that moment.

Hanae's stomach was still very uneasy, but she no longer felt as if she wanted to be physically sick, and the feeling of cleanliness helped a lot as she began to explore her surroundings. It became clear at once that the apartment was much too oddly-shaped to be in a block, and that she had no idea where she was. The bathroom had no windows anyway, being ventilated by an extractor fan which cut in automatically when the light was switched on. Next to it she found the kitchen, which was simple but equipped with a modern sink unit. This had a small window, but it was very dark outside and Hanae was unable to see any lights or even a skyline.

A digital clock perched on top of a small refrigerator indicated 4.45, and Hanae switched off the light to get a better impression of the outlook from the window. It was as she was blinking and adjusting her vision to the gloom that her heart lurched at the sound of a gentle cough behind her. Hanae spun round, her back to the sink, and sick terror filled her again as she realised that there was someone in the kitchen with her.

"I am glad you seem to be feeling better." The voice was that of a man. It had a thick, throaty quality, but obviously belonged to a person of good education. As he went on speaking Hanae became aware of the almost excessive politeness of the forms of address the man used, though the thudding of her heart and the shortness of her breath made it almost impossible for her to understand what he was saying. "It would probably have been possible to secure this apartment in such a way as to persuade the lady that any attempt to escape would be unsuccessful, and the idea of allowing for a preliminary period of solitary reflection had its attractions. However, personal supervision is simpler, and more effective.'

The figure approached, and Hanae shrank back helplessly as her forearm was grasped firmly. She could now see that the man had some kind of hood over his head, which made him all the more frightening. "Come, madam. Come and take a seat in the living room, where we can talk more comfortably." He gave her arm a sharp tug, and almost dragged her away from the sink. Moving confidently in the darkness the man led Hanae out of the kitchen and past the open screen door of the tatami room in which she had woken up.

The rest of the flat was obviously furnished in Western style, for Hanae felt her bare feet sink into the pile of a carpet as she was pulled after him, still weak and sick and terrified. Then the man turned and shoved her violently backwards. Her knees buckled and with a choking sob she fell back, into the softness of an armchair. "I do apologise for my impoliteness. I find myself behaving very discourteously lately."

Hanae opened her mouth to speak, but words would not come. It was with a sense of almost detached surprise that she heard a wailing, uncertain scream emerging from her own mouth, interspersed with frantic, jerking sobs, which continued for what seemed like an eternity until a burning, stinging pain grew in her face and she realised that the man was slapping her savagely. "Be silent! Silence!" There was real and obvious menace in the thick angry voice, and

103

Hanae cringed back, whimpering in pain and confusion. "If there is any repetition of that noise you will be gagged. That will make you feel a great deal worse, I assure you."

The figure looming over her was like a nightmare in its blackness, and Hanae became aware of an acrid fragrance, of male sweat mixed with the lingering hint of some kind of cologne which was not totally unfamiliar, though her husband never used anything of the kind. The man in the hood waited, then as she made no further sound moved away and slid open some inner shutters which revealed the outlines of wood-and-paper *shoji* screens like those in their house in Rokko. It was still dark outside, but enough light now filtered into the room for Hanae to be able to see that it contained a sofa and another armchair besides the one in which she was sitting.

Her captor made no attempt to switch on a light, but after hesitating for a moment, took the other armchair. "This need not take long," he said, reverting to his earlier gentlemanly manner. "I want to know where it is, that's all. You will of course have to remain here until it is safely in my hands, but after that there will be no reason to detain you further, and you may go home." He paused, and Hanae wearily raised her head, then jerked herself up as she realised that her yukata was gaping open to her waist. The sense of outraged modesty did more than anything to bring her to full consciousness, and she covered herself hurriedly. Her voice was wavering and uncertain, but at least she could now speak.

"Who are you, and what do you want? I cannot understand what you are talking about," she began, furious that the tears had begun to flow again. She mopped her eyes with the sleeve of her yukata and sniffed fiercely.

"I want to know where the netsuke is, my dear Mrs Otani. Please don't make me angry by pretending you know nothing about it. I have in my pocket the piece of paper on which you wrote the names of all nine, and I know quite well that you have discussed the matter with your husband.''

A terrible certainty began to take shape in Hanae's mind. The voice, the strange quality, phlegmy and hoarse: it sounded forced and unnatural, as though assumed. The last time any man apart from Otani had touched her had been when he took her arm to cross the road to the coffee house; and that was when she had caught the fragrance of that cologne and been tempted to ask the name of it.

She opened her eyes wide at the lean hooded figure in the shadows, and the smell of the cologne seemed very strong in her nostrils. Hanae just managed to whisper ''Ki . . . Kimura . . .'' before she passed out for the second time in less than eight hours.

Chapter XII

"**B**UT THERE MIGHT BE A PHONE MESSAGE, YOU see," Otani insisted, and his son-in-law Akira Shimizu sat back in his easy-chair and surveyed him in silence. Akiko was murmuring quietly to their small son in the bedroom which led directly off the Western-style living room of their cramped and crowded flat. It was almost as though the child had sensed and somehow understood the tension in the atmosphere, for he had submitted quietly to the routines of bathtime and bedtime with no more than a grave scrutiny of the grandfather who had for once dislodged him from the centre stage.

"That's about the tenth time you've said that," Shimizu pointed out patiently. "And I've explained over and over again that if you *do* get a call it will be either at Rokko or your office. We can quite see why you don't want to go back to Rokko alone, and in a way I can understand why you don't want us to move in with you for a while. Still, Inspector Kimura's arranged for a man to be on duty there throughout the day and night; and there's always someone to take a message at your headquarters. So long as your men know where to find you what does it matter? At least stay here overnight. You look terrible.''

Thank you,'' said Otani courteously, and managed a ghost of a smile. He was sitting in the only other armchair in the small room, a cushion behind his head and his bare feet resting on another placed on a low stool normally guarded with baleful jealously by his grandson Kazuo to whom it belonged. Through the fog of exhaustion and anxiety over Hanae he knew well enough that his mental and physical efficiency were at a very low ebb, and he wanted very much to allow the warmth and relaxation in his lower limbs to sweep up into his head and engulf him in oblivion.

It was curious how Shimizu seemed always to be able to winkle confidential information out of him, and even more curious that he trusted him so implicitly, this astute young business executive who a dozen or so years earlier had been the real brains behind the student rioting in Kobe and whom he had personally interrogated over endless bone-wearying hours between the set-piece battles with the tear-gas and water-cannons on the one side and the lengths of two-by-two wood and crude Molotov cocktails on the other. If anyone had told him in those days that his daughter would marry the brilliant, fanatical boy and that in the fullness of time he would himself be pouring out his perplexities to him, Otani would have quite simply fallen into one of his rare fits of uproarious laughter.

For his daughter Akiko it had been enough to see her father sagging at the door of her flat in mid-afternoon, his normally swarthy face pallidly yellow, and to hear Inspector Kimura's rapid muttered explanation that Mrs Otani was missing and the Superintendent had had no sleep. In the succeeding hours she had bullied him into eating and into taking a bath, astonishing herself by offering to wash him, a service she had performed, like most Japanese daughters, often enough in the past, but one which their liberated principles ruled out her offering to her husband; or his expecting. Not that Otani had accepted, having merely raised one eyebrow in tired surprise and shaken his head briefly.

Since Shimizu arrived home he had at least been talking, even though at first he had closed his eyes and shaken his head when pressed to think of any reason why Hanae might have disappeared. It had taken Shimizu a good hour of patient and oblique probing to elicit even part of the story of the netsuke, and even then he had failed to find out how his parents-in-law had come by it.

"No, I mean it. You really don't look in the least well," said Shimizu, then glanced away from Otani as the doorbell rang briefly.

Akiko appeared from the bedroom almost at once. "That will be Inspector Kimura," she said, hurriedly taking off her apron. "He said he'd be back at about eight." Shimizu stood up as Akiko opened the door. It was Kimura, and Otani grunted introductions from the depths of his chair as the two younger men bowed slightly to each other and Akiko ushered Kimura in.

When they were all sitting down Otani roused himself to speak, though his voice was hesitant and unsteady. "I have been meaning to arrange for you two to meet," he said. "Sorry it has to be under these circumstances. Thank you for coming back, Kimura. I'll get you to drop me at headquarters as soon as I get my clothes on. I'll be sleeping there for the time being."

Kimura opened his mouth to say something, then caught Shimizu's eye and shrugged his shoulders slightly. "Whatever you say, sir," he agreed.

"Sit down for a moment, though," Otani continued. "Tell us what you've found out." He closed his eyes, and Shimizu briefly explained to Kimura that since it had turned into a family affair, his father-in-law had confided to some extent in them.

Kimura was clearly uneasy, but in the absence of any help from Otani had no option but to report, and tried to do so in guarded terms. It was, of course, perfectly conventional Japanese practice to call a family council meeting to consider a serious problem; but when that problem related also to delicate police enquiries it made for an extraordinarily complicated situation.

"Well, sir," he began, addressing himself to the closed eyes of Otani as Akiko brought him a cup of green tea and a bean-jam cake which he acknowledged with a smile which quite unnerved her, "I wonder if it might not be easier to go into the details when Inspector Noguchi is available . . ."

One eye snapped open, and Otani's voice was hard. "I wish to have your report now."

Kimura hesitated, then plunged ahead. "Yes, well, very good, sir. As you instructed me to do, I have had a confidential message sent to all divisional and sectional offices and police boxes in the Kobe City and suburban area. Reports are in from almost all of them on the results of checking accident notifications and hospitals and private clinics." He paused. "All negative, but we may be sure that if any trace of Mrs Otani is picked up, we shall be informed at once."

Otani nodded heavily. "Keep it to our own prefecture for another twenty-four hours. After that if we haven't found her . . ."

" . . . We'll circulate a missing person notification nationally," Kimura supplied.

Otani nodded again. "What about Yago?" Even with his eyes shut he must have sensed Kimura's uneasy glance from one to the other of the Shimizus, because after a second he spoke again. "I said, what about Yago? Don't worry about my daughter and her husband." Kimura chewed on his lip for a moment, then with a mental shrug began to speak. There seemed to be nothing else for it.

"You asked me to check on the background and career of former General Kaori Yago. Fortunately the central reference library at headquarters still has all the old pre-war biographical handbooks, and I was able to piece together most of the essentials without too much trouble. I couldn't get at any of the accounts of the war crime tribunal, though. The National Diet Library has the complete archives and press reports of the period, of course, but I had to work with what we have here." He looked up at Akiko. "Do you mind if I smoke?" Her eyes wide, Akiko shook her head hurriedly and found an ashtray containing two brightly coloured plastic building bricks which she shook out into her hand before passing it to Kimura.

He lit a cigarette with a hand that was not perfectly steady, and continued. "The Yagos are a very well-connected family. The general's mother was in fact a daughter of one of the Emperor's own relatives. He had the usual education: Peer's School and Gakushuin University, then the Military Academy. Rapid promotion, especially after the February 26 mutiny, instructor at Military Academy, service in Manchuria." Kimura paused, and his next words dropped like pebbles into a quiet pool. "Was decorated after the Nanking Campaign, when he was a colonel, still in his thirties. Then nothing because there were no Army Lists published after the beginning of the Pacific War. Nothing on the military side. I was advised to check the Yago connection in civilian life, though, and found that he was quite active in setting up the so-called Yago Foundation for Asian Art. Quite a collector he was, especially in Manchuria."

He looked up. "The rest isn't conveniently documented and brings us up to much more recent times. I remember very vaguely from my own childhood the gossip at the time of the tribunals. People said General Yago was rather like the German one, Hitler's associate, what was his name?"

"Goering." It was Shimizu who supplied it. "Marshal Goering. Upper-class, connoisseur of the arts, stole a fortune in paintings and so on from European collections and had them shipped back to Germany."

"Yes, you're right," Otani said quietly in the following silence. "We did call him the Goering of Japan." He opened his eyes and focused on Kimura. "Family? Wife, children?"

Kimura shook his head. "Nothing much on the record. Married, one son. No details."

Otani rubbed a dry hand over his eyes. "We don't need them, do we? We know who the son is."

Shimizu looked enquiringly at Kimura, who shrugged visibly this time. "He's a member of the Diet—the Upper House. No mystery about it. In his forties. Married to a woman from this area, as a matter of fact, and has political support here." Otani sat up in his chair and took his feet off the stool. The effect was as though he had leapt to his feet.

"Who told you that?" he demanded. Kimura looked at him in some surprise.

"Why, Ninja Noguchi," he said. "That's why I suggested we should discuss the whole thing with him."

The eyes behind the puffy bags were cold and hard. "I do not wish to discuss this case with Inspector Noguchi," he said clearly and distinctly. "Nor do I wish you to discuss it with him, Kimura." With a painful effort he levered himself to his feet and stood there a little unsteadily in the small, crowded living room. "I'll go and put my clothes on," he announced, and disappeared into the bedroom, sliding the *fusuma* screen shut behind him.

Akiko, who had been standing behind her father throughout most of the conversation, gently and almost unconsciously massaging his neck and shoulders, flopped down into the vacant chair and looked at her husband. "What are we to do with him?" she asked rather plaintively. Then she turned to Kimura. "What on earth is all this business about a general supposed to mean?" This was the first Kimura had seen of the liberated, plain-speaking Akiko, and her manner was in sharp contrast to the troubled concern with which she had greeted him earlier in the day and her conventionally dutiful attentiveness to her

111

father subsequently. Now her eyes flashed and she almost snapped at him.

"Naturally, you must be very worried about your mother," he began awkwardly.

"Never mind my mother for the moment. Unless you can explain what this General Yagi . . ."

"Yago," said Shimizu. Not Yagi. Yago."

Akiko's glare was turned on her husband. "Never mind that. What I want to know is whether all that was relevant to anything, or whether my father is wandering in his mind or something."

Shimizu answered for Kimura. "No, he's not wandering. He's exhausted, and worried. But he's on to something, isn't he, Kimura-san?"

Kimura greatly enjoyed his own role as *enfant terrible* in relation to Otani, and experienced a pang of something he was honest enough to identify as being close to jealousy as he surveyed Akira Shimizu, a good ten years younger than himself and clearly enjoying much more of the confidence of his father-in-law than was usual for young Japanese husbands.

Shimizu seemed to sense Kimura's mood, because he went on very quietly, speaking directly to him. "I expect you know that I've good reason to respect Otani-san's ability. I was very close to him in a strange way long before I married my wife. It's obvious to me that my mother-in-law's disappearance is linked with this police business he's working on. The netsuke he told us about must be the connection to the Yago family. Now we learn that Yago's wife comes from this area. I begin to follow the lines of his thinking. You probably know already, Kimura-san."

All this was both unwelcome and confusing for Kimura, who wished devoutly to exclude the Shimizu couple from any deeper involvement. If the chief was going to continue ruminating aloud in their presence and to require him to present oral reports to the family circle, something had to be done. Tired as he was, the old man would probably function more satisfactorily in a police environment, and it would certainly be a lot less complicated for Kimura himself.

He avoided answering Shimizu by glancing at his watch. ''I wonder if the Superintendent will take long,'' he said enquiringly.

Akiko's eyes flashed again. ''I think it's quite ridiculous for him to leave here in this condition,'' she announced, then glanced round at the closed screen door. After a moment's hesitation, she stood up and went over to it. ''Father? Are you dressed yet?'' She tapped on the screen lightly, and when there was no reply, inched it open and peeped inside. Then she turned to the two men in the living room. ''Well, I don't know about tomorrow, but he's staying here tonight,'' she said firmly.

Shimizu raised an eyebrow, then stood up and went over to investigate. After a quick look inside the bedroom he turned to Kimura with a smile and beckoned him over. Otani was fast sleep, sprawled on the bedding which Akiko had laid out on the tatami matting earlier when settling their small son down on his own little mattress to one side. One of Otani's arms was stretched out protectively over his grandson. He had his trousers on, but had not yet taken off the cotton yukata he had been wearing. The effect was very odd.

Chapter XIII

MIGISHIMA HUNG BACK AS KIMURA LED THE WAY DOWN the carpeted staircase which led to the Love Box Cabaret, and Kimura glanced back and grinned at him encouragingly. Tired and worried as he was, he was quite looking forward to the next hour or so. "Don't look so depressed, Migishima," he said in a bantering voice. "Even if they do have the cheek to give us a bill at the end, we don't have to pay it ourselves." Migishima smiled wanly but said nothing, and Kimura shrugged and went on down.

The burly receptionist-cum-bouncer on duty at the street level entrance in his flashy dinner jacket must have passed the word downstairs, because as the two police officer entered the dimly-lit bar an older man came forward and bowed obsequiously. He too was dressed in fashionable evening clothes, and there was a faded refinement about his pale face with its long upper lip. His eyes avoided Kimura's as he greeted him extravagantly, while Migishima looked about them glumly.

The basement room was not of any great size. Dark red plush banquettes were ranged against the simulated wood

114

panelling of the walls, on which were hung a few oil paintings of an archly romantic nature, mostly depicting plump nude women with inviting smiles. There were a dozen or so small tables, with chairs upholstered in the same burgundy colour on the other side of them opposite the banquettes, and in the centre was a tiny dance floor with a revolving mirrored ball hung above it. This flashed multifaceted gleams of reflection from a rose-coloured spotlight trained on it. The other lighting was mainly from candles in glass shades on the tables. The recorded music which came over the loudspeakers was relatively quiet, and was characterised by massed strings with occasional chansons.

There were no more than half a dozen customers in the room, all attended by hostesses, only a few of whom seemed to be Japanese. Kimura and Migishima were ushered to a table some distance away from those already occupied, and a smart young waiter bustled over to them with small dishes of rice crackers and shredded dried squid, then stood deferentially awaiting their order. After a good deal of hesitation, Migishima opted for beer, while Kimura ordered Scotch on the rocks. Noticing a whispered conference at the bar involving the middle-aged manager, he was not surprised when the waiter returned with a new bottle of Chivas Regal and, after pouring Kimura a generous drink, left it open on the table in front of him. "Know how much this stuff costs?" Kimura asked Migishima as he raised the glass to his lips. Migishima shook his head. "Well, in the department store about fifteen thousand yen a bottle. Here, at the very least two thousand for a single. And they've given me the whole bottle."

"Perhaps they're worried," Migishima suggested, his eyes fixed sadly on his own very ordinary glass of beer. It was the first time he had spoken since he had received Kimura's call instructing him to meet him outside the cabaret at the unearthly hour of eleven-thirty at night.

Kimura shook his head. "Hardly. Just anxious to show their willingness to collaborate. Ah. Here come the girls."

He looked up and smiled expansively as Amanda Thorn-dike and Judy Cheng approached. Even for Kimura it was something of a surprise to see them in their working attire, while Migishima goggled foolishly at them, then blushed scarlet as they came close. Amanda was wearing a long black dress cut very low in the front to reveal most of her breasts, framed in a glittering diamanté border. Her hair was loose over her shoulders, and her make-up was that of a classic *femme fatale*. She slid on to the banquette close beside Migishima and seized his upper arm, revealing glitter-dust on the green shadow of her eyelids and a frilly garter on one elegant thigh as her dress parted almost to the hip.

Almost as much of Judy's legs was disclosed by the *cheongsam* of scarlet silk she was wearing, but its high Chinese tunic collar was in sharp contrast, leading the eye up to her neat regular facial features and the bell of perfectly arranged hair, then down again in the realisation that the high round breasts under the silk moved softly, unconfined by a bra.

"Well hello again, Inspector Nacker," Amanda crooned in English, to Kimura's confusion. Again that mysterious word *nacker* which he had not had time to look up.

"Kimura," he said a little sharply. "This is one of my assistants. Detective Migishima. He doesn't speak English. Where are the other two?"

Amanda looked round casually, then treated Migishima to a huge carnivorous smile culminating in a pursing of her brightly painted lips in a combination of kiss and pout, before replying. "Busy, darling. We're popular girls, you know. You can't just ring up and expect us to be at your beck and call exactly when you specify. Nancy's over there, with those two old buffers in the corner. And Hélène's . . . out." Kimura glanced in the direction indicated, and saw Nancy Berstein in animated conversation with an elderly man with silver hair. His companion was a man of about the same age, but who had dyed his own hair jet black, and who sat back with a bored expression on his face as the other two talked. Nancy too was dressed in an ostensibly seductive style, in high-fashion jeans and a see-through blouse, but her manner was impatient rather than languourous. Amanda raised an eyebrow. "Don't understand what they see in her? Not your type, definitely, darling," she said, leaning across Migishima to address Kimura directly. Migishima cringed as a wave of perfume engulfed him.

Kimura spoke seriously. "Look, this is important," he said. "An emergency, you might say. I need your cooperation, and there isn't time for foolery."

Amanda's mouth snapped open. "OK. Start talking," she said crisply. "But don't upset the other customers. One or two people are noticing you as it is." She smiled lecherously at Migishima and fondled his hand, while Judy took the hint and started nibbling the lobe of Kimura's ear.

Kimura switched the conversation to Japanese, and found that both girls spoke it fairly well and appeared to understand it even more. The businesslike nature of the conversation was in bizarre contrast to the gropings and squeezings which accompanied it as Amanda and Judy moved into their practised routines. Kimura was too old a hand to be greatly distracted, but there were several moments when a glazed look came over Migishima's face, and at one point he uttered a startled squawk and pulled away from Amanda, earning himself a withering rebuke from Kimura.

The waiter brought several rounds of drinks for the girls and Kimura was about a quarter of the way through the bottle of Chivas Regal when the middle-aged manager approached, having put down the telephone receiver into which he had been speaking. Hovering some paces away, he coughed discreetly, and Kimura disentangled himself from Judy's embrace and stood up to talk to him, then nodded and crossed to the phone.

By the time he returned Judy had moved in on Migishima as well, and Kimura gazed with some amusement at

117

the brick-red face of his assistant, framed as it was by those of the English and the Chinese girl, who were both whispering ardently into his slightly oversized ears. "I've got to go, Migishima," he said, then gestured to him to remain when Migishima began to struggle to free himself. "No. You stay here. I think we were beginning to get somewhere, and it looks as if Nancy-san will be able to join you before long." He turned on his heel and left the Love Box Cabaret, pausing only to give some brief instructions to the manager, and unsure whether or not he had heard Migishima groan gently as the two girls returned to the attack.

Chapter XIV

THE DIRECTOR AND THE CURATOR OF THE MUSEUM IN Kyoto were both in attendance with Otani and Kimura swept in during the afternoon of the following day, and the style of Otani's second visit was sharply different from that of the first. He was in uniform, and he was expected, having ordered Kimura to arrange the visit with the full knowledge and collaboration of the Kyoto Prefectural Police. Otani said nothing as he suffered himself to be led once more to the Director's office, and rather than bowing gave a stiff and, to those present, alien salute by way of greeting. He then removed his goldbraided cap and sat bolt upright in the chair indicated.

Kimura, who was in formal civilian dress, which suited his pale face and the dark shadows under his eyes, went through more conventional Japanese courtesies and murmured perfunctory apologies for the intrusion; but on instructions from Otani made little attempt to soften the chilly formality of the occasion. The two Museum officials took seats opposite Otani and Kimura, and complete silence prevailed while handleless cups of green tea were brought in

119

and placed before them. Kimura had seen Otani's face as set and grim as it now was on many occasions over the years, and was relieved to note that the puffy exhaustion and dull hopelessness of the previous day seemed to have disappeared. In the eyes was a look with which Kimura was not familiar, though, and it worried him. There was a glitter which was far from healthy or natural, and Otani's stillness was not a matter of relaxation but of tense rigidity.

The Director looked enquiringly at Otani, who remained mute, then turned to the obviously more approachable Kimura and cleared his throat. "I very much regret," he began unhappily, "any impression which we may have given of reluctance to co-operate to the fullest possible extent in police enquiries, or of being over-zealous in seeking custody of the object which the Superintendent discussed with my colleague the Curator recently."

Otani inclined his head curtly in acceptance of the apology, and unbent minimally. He opened his mouth to speak, and looked directly at the Curator, who was sitting in dignified silent despair, no doubt pondering the best timing for his resignation. "I have no complaint about the trend of the discussion during my last visit," he said coldly. "Your colleague here received me with personal courtesy, and was helpful and informative. It is natural that he should have been professionally anxious to ensure that the netsuke I showed him should be placed in expert hands as soon as possible. I have made it clear at the highest level in Tokyo that the police authorities have no wish to retain custody longer than necessary. I am sure the object will be handed over to you before long. You should not reproach yourselves."

There was a perceptible lightening of the atmosphere, and the Curator drank his tea in a single huge gulp. Otani sipped his own, then continued. "You can hasten the process of the investigation significantly by giving us some confidential technical assistance."

As soon as the Director heard this, he began to nod with

120

enthusiasm. "Anything, of course, our facilities are at your disposal . . ." he babbled, and Otani cut in smoothly, gesturing to Kimura.

"Please explain, Inspector," he said, then relapsed into his former silence.

Kimura took out a notebook. "I would stress the word 'confidential' which the Superintendent used," he said. "I will explain. We must have detailed photographs of the seven pieces of the set which are in the collection of this Museum. We would prefer these to be taken by a police photographer, but it would be simpler and quicker if the work could be done in your own laboratory. I imagine you have high-magnification photographic equipment?"

The Curator nodded, becoming more cheerful by the minute. "Of course. And we have a most trustworthy technician, not that it would be anything out of the ordinary for me to ask him to undertake such a task."

Kimura nodded slightly. "Where are the seven pieces kept when they aren't on show?"

Instead of replying immediately, the Curator rose to his feet and looked down at the three other men. "I think it would be best if we go to the strong room now, then you can explain how best we can be of assistance."

"Yes," Otani said decisively, and they all stood up.

At the door the Director held back. "Ah, as you know, Superintendent," he began awkwardly, "I am an administrative civil servant, not a technical expert . . . unless you feel I can contribute anything . . ."

Otani looked him up and down. "I have no doubt of your discretion, Director," he said. "However, in principle the fewer people involved the better. I am obliged to you." Then he swept out in the direction indicated by the Curator, who led him and Kimura to a battered goods lift in which they descended into the basement.

Casting a professional eye over the visible security arrangements, Kimura was moderately impressed, and the Curator noticed his interest. "It's not like keeping money

121

in a bank,'' he explained as an attendant unlocked an iron grille to admit them to yet another musty concrete corridor. ''Of course we have to consider the possibility of theft in the actual galleries, but down here most of our responsibilities are concerned with conservation and controlling humidity, temperature and exposure to light.'' He twiddled the dial of a combination lock on a steel door in front of them, then chose a key from a ring in his pocket and fitted it into one of the two keyholes. The attendant provided the second, and the heavy door swung open to admit them to a strong room lined with steel cabinets.

With yet another key the Curator opened one and took out a polished wooden case which he placed on an open shelf while he relocked the cabinet. Then he turned to Otani and Kimura. ''The light in here is poor,'' he said, opening the flat case and displaying its contents, ''but before we go to the laboratory I will show you that right from the beginning we hoped one day to have all nine.'' The box was beautifully made and fitted with nine recesses, the whole being lined with red velvet. In seven of them nestled buxom ivory goddesses, leaving the other two looking oddly bereft. At the base of each niche was a small plastic name-plate, and Kimura's eyes widened as he bent to take a closer look at them. He made as if to say something, then thought better of it and stood aside to make way for Otani, who gave the contents of the box only a cursory glance.

As the three men made their way out of the strong room the Curator tucked the case almost casually under his arm while he and the attendant relocked the steel door, and then preceded them out through the grille and along another corridor until he stopped outside a door labelled ''Research Room''; one of the several so described. It was a bare little room, containing a battered wooden table with two upright chairs, and a bench along one wall with a cupboard mounted above. The general level of lighting was bright, and there was a spotlamp on the table.

The Curator gestured to the two chairs, and dragged a

122

stool from the bench for himself, then opened the box again so that all three of them could see inside at the same time.

"I see you have names for them, including the missing ones," said Kimura casually. "How can you tell which is which?"

The Curator looked surprised, and answered readily. "Well, they each have the appropriate name carved on them, so it's quite obvious," he said. "As you see, we have them printed on these labels in Greek, *katakana* phonetic Japanese and English."

"So the missing ones must be Thalia and Clio?" The question came quietly from Otani, and startled Kimura, who had assumed that Otani would be unable to read the Roman script and would not make the necessary deduction from the clumsy Japanese phonetic approximation *Kureio*.

The Curator nodded. "Undoubtedly. The names of all nine Muses are well-known and recorded in countless places, and we certainly have the other seven here."

A spot of colour had appeared in each of Otani's cheeks, and Kimura thought he could see him quivering slightly. "A magnifying glass, please," he said and the curator went to the cupboard and produced a large one. Taking it in his left hand, Otani lifted one of the netsuke out of its padded recess and studied it briefly. Putting it back, he selected a second, and then a third and so on until he had looked at all seven under the glass, taking no more than a few seconds over each. Putting the last one back, he sat back with a little sigh and rubbed his eyes.

Then he looked at the Curator. "Yes," he said heavily. "Can you use the magnifying camera yourself?" The Curator nodded a little uncertainly. "I need only one picture of each," Otani continued, closing the box gently. "If you will show me how to focus on any particular feature, I should be grateful if I may take the pictures myself under your supervision." His face softened briefly in a weary smile. 'Your cooperation this morning is much appreciated. I think we may have found what we hoped."

* * *

As Tomita drove them back to Kobe along the toll road Kimura remained silent for as long as he could in deference to Otani's manifest desire to avoid conversation, reflecting on the adroit way he had managed to photograph each of the seven Museum netsuke while concealing from the Curator the aspect in focus. And now the roll of film reposed in Otani's pocket and the National Treasures were back in the strong room. Eventually Kimura could bear it no longer.

"With respect, sir, you can't develop the film yourself. And it won't take long for that expert to put them under high magnification himself and see whatever is to be seen."

"I expect you're right on both counts," Otani said quite equably. "In fact I want you to supervise the development yourself. I want one set of enlargements, and the negatives. No further copies. As to the second, we'll see. You didn't hear what I said to him while he was putting them away." It was true. Kimura had been irritated at being instructed to remain in the so-called Research Room while Otani and the Curator took the netsuke back through the grille.

Tomita made reasonably good time along the highway, and they were back at headquarters shortly before six. In the entrance hall Otani handed the film over to Kimura, who bore it off in the direction of the small studio and darkroom installation at the back of the building, then made his way slowly up the broad stairs and along the familiar corridor with the strip of coconut matting on the shiny brown linoleum. He paused at the last of the formal framed photographs which lined the walls. All Otani's predecessors were there, depicted with grim, forbidding expressions. Even those of recent years had a Victorian look to them, and it had more than once crossed Otani's mind to write a little monograph about them one day. In his exhaustion he stood and gazed for a moment at the space where within a few years at most his own photograph would hang; then moved on and went into his office.

On his desk was a small pile of papers, on the top of

which was a plain white envelope with his name and title typed neatly on it, and Otani slit it open incuriously and took out a slip of paper, small enough not to need to be folded. He caught his breath as he read the typed message, and immediately reached out a hand to press the buzzer on his telephone. Just as he did so the instrument rang, and he picked up the receiver instead. "Personal call for you, sir," said the switchboard operator briskly, and there followed a click then silence. "Yes? Otani here."

"You've read the message, I trust," said a thick male voice. "Now listen. The connection will be broken in seconds, so don't waste time trying to trace it." The blood pounded in Otani's head as he heard then Hanae's voice. "Tetsuo . . . darling. I'm alright. I don't know where I am, but I'm not hurt . . ." Another click and the line was dead.

For perhaps a quarter of an hour Otani sat slumped at his desk, sick with mingled relief and frustration, then a terrible anger rose up in him as he summoned the senior duty officer, who happened to be Inspector Sakamoto, and who stood at ramrod attention under the onslaught, as bitter as it was unprecedented. His regulation-bound mind reeled in the effort to understand why he was being rebuked and what he was being ordered to do, and when the door opened to admit Kimura with a large envelope in his hand and Otani abruptly broke off his tirade, Sakamoto still stood stiff and silent.

Otani looked from one to the other of the inspectors. "Dismissed!" he barked at Sakamoto, who turned on his heel and marched from the room, a dazed expression on his face.

Kimura hesitated, half inclined to follow Sakamoto, then closed the door quietly behind him and approached the desk where Otani sat breathing heavily. "What happened?" Kimura's question was abrupt and authoritative, and as he asked it he was beginning to wonder if he might have to

125

take the dire step of reporting his commander to be unfit to carry out his duties.

Otani's mouth worked for a few seconds before he answered. "She spoke to me, Kimura," he muttered at last. "Telephone. Cut off. And this . . ." He pushed the piece of paper on his desk an inch or two in Kimura's direction.

"I see. You wanted Sakamoto to account for its delivery."

Otani nodded once. "And the phone call. Personal, they said. Trace should be made automatically."

Kimura breathed deeply, and nodded in agreement. "I'll look into it, sir. I doubt if Sakamoto was quite clear about the problem. At least we have something to work on now. An anonymous note demanding that the netsuke should be handed over by this time tomorrow, and the call from Mrs Otani."

Otani raised a hand wearily. "No. From the writer. Must have been watching us come back here. Knew exactly when I would read it. Then my wife, a few words."

Kimura realised that Otani might have heard a tape-recording, and knew equally that if he were to suggest the possibility it would mean the end of rational conversation. "I'll find out how the note was delivered," he promised. "And needless to say, I'll make sure that any further unidentified calls for you are traced." He paused, then leaned over the edge of the desk. "Why not hand the thing over, sir? It looks as though it really would get Mrs Otani released, and surely we have enough of a lead now to push this case through after she's safe."

Kimura was surprised by the look of despair which came through as Otani shook his head. "I can't contemplate that for the moment," he said. "I can't tell you why." Then he looked at the envelope Kimura was still holding in one hand. "Well?"

Still unable to imagine why Otani seemed indecisive about the terms for his wife's release, Kimura opened the envelope and took out a set of enlargements of the pictures

Otani had taken. They were still slightly damp from processing, and he peeled them apart carefully and laid them out on the desk in front of Otani. "You did a good job, sir," he said truthfully.

The pictures were indeed sharp and clear, bringing out not only the delicate cross-hatching of the old ivory, but showing quite clearly the nature of the markings which had been concealed on each one in roughly the same position as those on the netsuke Hanae had found in the Hotel Fantasia. Otani brooded over the prints in silence for a while, then began to push them about to alter their relative positions, almost as though he were playing a game of solitaire with playing cards. Then he looked up at Kimura.

"You know almost as much as I do now," he said slowly. "Letters and figures, and we don't even know what order they're supposed to be in. What now, Kimura? I'm too tired to think."

"It's a fantastic lead!" Kimura tried hard to convey enthusiasm. "Obviously there's a message here, and we can get the cryptanalysts in the Defence Agency to help us crack it if necessary . . ."

"Seven-ninths of a message, more likely. There are nine in the set."

"Well, in that case, eight-ninths—don't forget the one you've got. I'm no expert, but I'm sure it will give them enough to go on."

Otani sat hunched over for a moment longer, then abruptly pushed himself upright and stood, then went over to the window. Kimura almost failed to hear what he said with his back turned, and could hardly believe what he did catch. He hurried over and looked Otani straight in the eye. "Can you *trust* me? Has it really come to that?"

Otani held the stare for several seconds, then dropped his eyes. "I do, Kimura. I must, and I do. I don't have the eighth netsuke. My wife hid it. I don't know where."

Kimura nodded slowly. "I see. Yes. That complicates

things. Look, sir, let me get Ninja in. He wants to see you urgently anyway . . ."

"No." Otani's voice was little more than a whisper, but it made Kimura's mouth snap shut. "This has to be done without Noguchi. I can't . . . you see . . . Kimura, for God's sake get me a drink.

Chapter XV

"**D**ON'T JUST SIT THERE," KIMURA SNAPPED. "I'M seriously worried about him, and you obviously know a hell of a lot more than you're saying." He glared across at Noguchi, who was wedged awkwardly into the inadequate chair behind the decrepit little desk in the cubby-hole of an office allotted to him on the ground floor. It was nearly eight in the evening and headquarters was quiet, except for the men in the main duty room on the other side of the building.

"Where is he now?" Noguchi spoke quietly, ignoring Kimura's manner.

"In his office, drinking whisky."

Noguchi raised an eyebrow. "Whisky? Not like him."

Kimura leaned forward. "Look, Ninja, the state he's in, it will probably be the best thing if he passes out cold. I don't know what you've said or done to him, but he won't see you. He'd probably half-kill me if he knew I was down here with you now. Now please, I beg you, tell me what you know about all this."

Noguchi moved one beefy hand slightly, as though about

to brush a fly away. "He did give it to his wife, then. Must hand it over. Only thing to do."

"It is connected with the Ventura murder, isn't it?" Kimura pressed, and Noguchi nodded once. "Ninja, what is your interest in all this? Can't you see, man, you're making me almost as suspicious as the chief is?"

Noguchi raised his head and for the first time scowled back in anger. "Shut your mouth, Kimura," he snarled. "My interest is, first, finding her and getting her out. Second, pinning the Ventura killing down."

"You know who did it?"

"Almost sure."

"Is it Yago?"

Noguchi ignored the question, extricated himself from his chair and lumbered over to the door. From there he surveyed Kimura expressionlessly. "Go back to him," he said at last. "His wife has got to tell them where it is. Make him see it's the only way."

Kimura tried once more. "Ninja. Yago . . . We're not fools, you know. I had a message from an inspector in the Met in Tokyo last night. Yago hasn't been at his Diet Building office for several days. I've had his house down there checked, and there's nobody there except a maid . . ." Kimura abandoned the sentence uncompleted as Noguchi turned his back on him and disappeared along the corridor.

On his way back to Otani's room Kimura passed his own office, to find Migishima there, half in and half out of the door in an attitude of suspense. A look of relief spread over his amiable face as Kimura approached.

"Oh. Migishima. I'd forgotten about you. Anything to report?" He brushed past the young man and sat at his own desk. "Quickly. I'm very busy at the moment. Sit down, do. There isn't time to be formal." He felt snappy and irritable, but something in Migishima's earnest eyes forced him to wait quietly as he sat on the edge of the hard chair on the other side of the desk, looming over Kimura.

"Sir," he began. "I stayed at the bar until they closed. Between them the three women produced four addresses where the Ventura woman might have gone with regular clients—apart from the Fantasia Hotel. There was another love hotel she used to use, and . . . I was surprised . . . two luxury flats owned by foreign diplomats . . ."

"You have a note of all these?" Kimura was both interested to learn this fact and even in his distracted state slightly annoyed that Migishima rather than he himself had come by it.

Migishima nodded. "The fourth is another luxury flat. I had difficulty in finding out who owns it, but eventually traced it back to the manager of the cabaret. But he doesn't live there: Apparently it's maintained for the use of special guests of the group who own the cabaret—and the Fantasia Hotel. What stuck in my mind especially was that the English girl—Amanda-san—said she had been there herself, with a man whose name she didn't know but must have been important. She said something odd. That she wouldn't buy a used car from him. Then she said he wore one of those badges like the big politicians you see on the TV news. Well, I thought at once that it might be a Dietman, but, sir, there are hundreds of them."

Kimura nodded in silence, trying to keep the excitement out of his expression. "So?"

"I, er, that is, you were in Kyoto with the Superintendent and so I took it upon myself to go to the flat this morning. There was no answer when I rang. I . . . I effected an entrance." Kimura could not restrain a quick grin as Migishima manfully brought out the still Police Handbook phraseology. "There was nobody there at all. But the place was fitted up very . . . er exotically." Migishima finally floundered to an embarrassed halt, and appeared to be waiting stoically for criticism or a rebuke.

It did not come. Kimura heaved a great sigh, then spoke warmly and unpatronisingly. "Unorthodox, perhaps, but you've done extremely well, Migishima. I'm only sorry

131

there wasn't anybody there, but you've provided valuable corroboration. For the moment do nothing else. Above all, don't make any further contact with any of the cabaret people until I let you know. Are you on late duty tonight?"

Migishima shook his head. "I was going to leave after reporting to you." He blushed. "Actually, my er, that is, Terauchi-san comes off duty at ten and I was going to see her home . . ."

Kimura looked at his watch. "Well, don't wait after that. I may have a job for you before then, though." He stood and went to the door. "Make yourself comfortable in here if you like," he said as he turned to go.

Otani was still at his desk in the position in which Kimura had left him, staring unseeingly at the photographs. Kimura was relieved to see that no more than a quarter of the bottle of Suntory whisky he had brought had been drunk, and that the glass at Otani's side was half full, evidently with a good deal of water added to the liquor. He looked up Kimura approached, and focused his stare. "I've decided to suspend Noguchi from duty," he said. "Is Sakamoto still in charge of the duty room? I want Noguchi arrested as a material witness."

Kimura was aghast, and his mouth opened and closed as he sought for words. "Sir, please listen to me," he pleaded at last. "I don't know what it is you suspect about Ninja—about Inspector Noguchi. But I'm convinced he's working with you, not against you. Please trust him—trust us both. He's desperately concerned about Mrs Otani's safety." He stared into Otani's stony face, willing him to believe. "Take him into your confidence, sir. Please. He has asked to see you. Maybe he *does* know something vital. Why in the world not let him tell you?"

"Tell me that he killed the Ventura woman?" Otani's voice was coldly level. "Not very likely."

"*What?* You don't seriously think that! Chief, you must not say things you'll regret—"

"Don't give me orders, Kimura. You'll do as I say, not

132

the other way round.'' Otani was still speaking in a quiet contained way, and Kimura backed off, sick with the conviction that his mind had cracked under the strain. Otani watched him carefully, and seemed to read his thoughts. ''Kimura, I'm in possession of my faculties,'' he said. ''I will tell you in confidence what I suspect, and you will then do as I say. The link between the Ventura woman and Noguchi is Manila. I didn't know this myself until recently, but he was there during the war. He caught sight of the netsuke on my desk, and quite obviously recognised it . . . Kimura, listen to what I say. I am *not* taking leave of my senses!'' In fact Kimura was not looking at Otani but at the photographs on the desk, and a strange expression had come into his face.

''Sir, I am listening,'' he protested, almost absent-mindedly. ''But wait please. This may be important. Manila. Please . . . may I just check something?'' Without waiting for permission he picked up the telephone and dialled his own internal extension number. ''Migishima? Kimura here. Quick; atlas on top of my locker. Map reference for Manila . . . *Manila* . . . you've heard the word often enough lately, man . . . yes, I know it's not very detailed . . .'' He listened for a while, then briefly thanked Migishima and rang off. Then he reached across and turned the photographs to face him, rearranging the order as he did so, pursing his lips reflectively.

When he spoke it was heavily, as though consciously avoiding any note of satisfaction or optimism. ''I don't know, sir, but I think you may have hit on the key to the message. I don't think it's a code at all; simply a grid reference. Just from the simple atlas I've got downstairs, it seems that Manila is about 14 degrees north and 122 east. The figures in these photos don't help much, but the only letters are N and E. We can get a precise grid reference easily enough, and see if we can shuffle these into any sort of order. Or maybe there's an accepted order of precedence for these Greek goddesses anyway . . .''

There was no doubt that Otani was listening. His eyes were glittering and his mouth was set in a small grim smile. "Get Noguchi," he said, and seemed to be on the point of adding something when the telephone shrilled, seemingly louder than usual. For a fraction of a second the two men hesitated, then reached for it simultaneously. Otani got there first, and Kimura watched his fist tighten round the receiver clamped to his ear. He could hear nothing of what was said, but stood stock-still by his own count of about half a minute until there was an audible click and Otani very slowly replaced the receiver, having said nothing.

At that moment the door crashed open and everything happened at once. Noguchi burst in, and simultaneously Otani shot out of his chair, his face contorted with fury, and flung himself at Noguchi. There could only be one outcome, and by the time Kimura got to them Nougchi had already pinioned Otani's arms. Otani was still hacking savagely at Noguchi's legs and Noguchi himself was breathing with difficulty but managed a hoarse shout which Kimura understood. Very deliberately he smacked Otani viciously across the face and Otani, momentarily stunned, drooped in Noguchi's grasp.

"Stop it!" Kimura's voice was loud and commanding. "Ninja traced the call! *We know where she is!*"

Gradually Noguchi released Otani, who rubbed his face, bright red from Kimura's blow, the insane rage of his former expression giving way to a dazed but more rational appearance.

Kimura was still glaring at him, and waited a few seconds until he was sure he had Otani's attention. "You can apologise to Ninja later," he then said, his own voice choked and unsteady with anger. "Come on!"

Chapter XVI

THE TERROR HANAE HAD FELT IN THE FIRST HOURS after regaining consciousness had faded somewhat as the area of the unknown diminished and she was able to understand at least dimly the circumstances in which she found herself. She was also feeling physically better, and her captors obviously did not plan to deprive her of food and drink. The biggest single factor in raising her spirits was the fact that she was able to detect tensions and differences between the two of them.

The man who had first terrified her by appearing hooded in the darkness had still not revealed his face, but Hanae had been overwhelmingly relieved to realise after she regained consciousness for the second time and as the hours wore on that he could not be Kimura, and that the thick, throaty voice in which he spoke was natural to him.

Although the small living-room was heavily curtained, enough light filtered through for Hanae to judge that it must be mid-morning when the woman who had first attacked her entered the room. She also wore a hood of dark material, but it looked more ridiculous than sinister on her.

For a few seconds she murmured into the man's ear, drawing the hood up at one side to do so, while Hanae sat utterly still in an attempt to overhear what was said. She had for the past half an hour been listening for any sound of movement above or below the room, having almost decided to gamble everything on one despairing scream for help before being overpowered again and gagged; but she had heard nothing.

Then it was suddenly too late. All at once the man got up, crossed to her and clamped a hand over her mouth. Hanae gave a muffled moan, then bit the hand as hard as she could, and had the satisfaction of hearing him grunt in pain; but then the woman had come to his assistance and Hanae was rapidly gagged with a square of silk of the kind used for wrapping awkward packages. Sickening though it was to feel the material across her tongue and pulling at the sides of her mouth, Hanae had time to experience a flash of ludicrous regret that the material would probably be ruined. Next, her arms were pulled roughly behind her and tied at the wrists with another *furoshiki* silk square.

The reason for these actions became apparent to Hanae when the man left the room, leaving her under the eye of the woman, who seemed to feel that some explanation might be called for. She even began by apologising.

"Look, I'm sorry," she said, in the cultivated, elegant voice of the previous evening, though a little unsteadily. "We didn't think it would be necessary to keep you here this long. Just tell me where you put the netsuke, that's all. Once we have it you can go." Hanae rolled her eyes helplessly. There was enough light in the room for her facial expression to be seen, and the woman went on. "We put the gag on to warn you what will happen if you scream or try to attract attention. I'll take it off so that you can talk if you agree not to make a noise. Nod if you agreed."

Hanae at once nodded vigorously. It was the first occasion since her schooldays that she had been subjected to physical abuse, and she felt the heaving sensations begin-

136

ning in her stomach again. Totally unprepared as she had been for the frightening events of the past night, though, she was sufficiently clear-headed to be struck by the amateurishness of the woman's assumption that in conditions of duress Hanae might, as it were, give her word of honour and abide by it. Almost at once the woman untied the gag, and Hanae panted with relief.

Then she found her voice. It was rather hoarse, which made it all the easier for Hanae to dissemble convincingly. "I already said—to him—over and over again, I don't know anything about netsuke. I don't know why you're doing this to me or what it's all about. Look, please untie my arms. I feel sick and you must realise I can't possibly defend myself against you. And . . . I'm thirsty and . . ." The last words were said with complete sincerity and Hanae's lip trembled. The tears which had come several times already welled up in her eyes and seemed to strike a sympathetic chord in her captor, who hesitated but finally untied Hanae's wrists.

As the day dragged on and darkness fell again a strange kind of camaraderie seemed to develop between the two women. Hanae was allowed to make herself some buttered toast and instant coffee, which she managed to keep down; and later on to prepare a bowl of instant noodles by pouring boiling water on them in their plastic container. The woman in the hood watched her eat, but took nothing herself. Finding the effect of the hood oppressive anyway, Hanae timidly suggested that she should take it off so as to be able to eat, pointing out that she had seen her face the previous evening anyway and was unlikely to forget it. The moment she said this Hanae realised that she would have been far better advised to imply the opposite, especially as her attempt at persuasion had no effect beyond a brief hardening of the woman's manner to her.

Even so, Hanae was allowed to use the bathroom in privacy before being ordered back into the bedroom. Time seemed to develop a strange elasticity. Earlier, a quarter of

137

an hour had seemed to take all eternity to elapse, yet in the darkness of the bedroom she fell almost at once into a heavy sleep, waking again in disoriented terror what seemed only minutes later to find that it was already day again. She felt weak and cold inside, but the nausea had passed.

When she stumbled out of the bedroom Hanae thought at first with a small thrill of hope that she was alone, but she was pushed back down into dull fear when the man emerged from the kitchen, adjusting the hood over his head as he approached her. He stopped as she stood there swaying slightly. The sinister, sightless head moved speculatively. It was as though he was wondering quite unemotionally whether a soft or hard approach would be the most effective, before opting for the former. "You may go to the kitchen," he said. "Eat and drink. Then talk."

It was only more toast and more coffee, but Hanae felt stronger as she obeyed the man's gesture after she had finished, and went back to the armchair. As the relentless inquisition was resumed she became more spirited and defiant in her responses, until she noticed his hands. The fingers seemed to have taken on a life of their own, and Hanae felt fear coming back to the point that it was a relief when the sound of a key in the lock was followed by the reappearance of the woman.

They went to a corner of the room and spoke in an undertone, seeming to be arguing about something. There was menace in the man's manner as he approached Hanae again, and she was too frightened and confused to resist when he again tied her wrists behind her before leaving her once more in the woman's charge. No more than ten minutes after his departure the woman made a small gesture of exasperation and released Hanae again. As much out of relief as anything, Hanae was careful to say nothing which would show her as being other than passive, intimidated and bewildered.

Once or twice during the second long day Hanae thought she might have heard sounds underneath, but was not sufficiently convinced to raise an outcry. For all she knew, her captors might have accomplices elsewhere in the building: certainly they seemed to come and go freely enough.

From time to time, usually with signs of reluctance as though following unwelcome instructions, the woman returned to the subject of the netsuke, using a variety of approaches ranging from sweet reason to obscure threats. These had little effect on Hanae, unlike the much more frightening techniques of the man. As the day wore on she had little difficulty in maintaining her attitude of bewildered ignorance, and eventually the desultory interrogation lapsed. Hanae sat slumped in the chair in the living room, gathering strength of mind as she realised that the woman was not only evidently tired but also increasingly jumpy and nervous. It was almost as though the tables were in an odd way turned, and Hanae was keeping an eye on the other woman.

As she sat there quietly, Hanae tried to push the sense of her own predicament into the background and to try to formulate some sort of theory which would account for the behaviour of this person of about her own age. Her composure on the first evening, when embarking on an enterprise Hanae was more and more convinced was alien to her, had been remarkable. She had sustained the role of the collector for the Society for Helping Handicapped Koreans with perfect assurance. Hanae had no idea whether there actually existed such a society: it seemed entirely likely. The ease and authority of her bearing was a matter of breeding and education, which was presumptive evidence that the woman was unlikely to be a professional criminal. Because she took an interest in current affairs and partly because years before she had tried very hard to understand the political motivations of her daughter Akiko, Hanae knew that extremism and even terrorism seemed, extraordinarily, to attract not only women as well as men, but women of the bourgeoisie at that. The enigma of the netsuke seemed to have no political coloration, though, and

139

the woman who first assaulted and now stood guard over her neither looked nor talked like a committed activist.

Although Hanae could not see her expression, she remembered the woman's face very well, and, staring at her now through half-closed eyes, something about the tension of her body made it quite easy to imagine a look of nervous anticipation in the well-cared-for features. The woman continually glanced at the watch on her wrist, and her whole body sagged with relaxation when there was the sound of footsteps on stairs outside the door and the man came back into the flat, still arranging his own hood round his neck, having obviously just put it on again. This time he made no attempt to prevent Hanae from hearing what he said to his accomplice.

The phlegmy voice was hot and angry. "What did you untie her for? How do you know she can be trusted?" Hanae was bemused by this second curious assumption that in her predicament she might be thought to be subject to normal considerations of moral obligation.

Her bemusement was short-lived, and was replaced by fear and anger when the man approached her and without warning slapped her savagely across the face. Immediately after that he seized her upper arms and dragged her from the chair in which she had been sitting. Hanae saw the glitter of the eyes through the openings in the mask, then the head was turned as he ordered the other woman to fetch the gag again. Hanae had long since concluded that she must be his wife, and the coarseness of his manner towards her confirmed it without the slightest possibility of doubt. Her face hot and stinging from the blow, Hanae struggled ineffectually as the gag was retied.

Then came the greatest insult of all. Suddenly the man dragged Hanae's cotton kimono down off her shoulders, and when she was naked to the waist quickly tied her wrists behind her with the loose sleeves. Even in her outrage she heard the quick intake of breath from the other woman and the beginnings of a protest from her, cut short by another

140

angry order from him. For a woman of Hanae's generation the mere fact of nudity was nothing to get particularly excited about, and as a child and throughout her puberty she had been quite accustomed to being naked in the presence of men in communal baths. Even in modern times nudity in the family tended to be taken for granted in spite of the fact that the old mixed baths at hot spring resorts had almost disappeared since the years of the American occupation.

It had been a good many years since Hanae had been seen in the nude by anybody but her husband, but she was not in the least ashamed of her body, which, if now perhaps a few pounds heavier than it might have been, was shapely and unblemished—it was the experience of being forcibly stripped which shocked and outraged her, being associated as it was in the Japanese mind solely with violence, cruelty and rape. Unlike some of the Western women Hanae occasionally read about in the detective stories Otani was forever buying, Hanae emphatically disliked the idea of being undressed by a man, and couldn't imagine a Japanese woman who would feel otherwise.

Physically distressed by the gag in her mouth and the lingering pain in her face, and shaken and disgusted by the treatment to which she was being subjected, Hanae cowered back in a mixture of fury and fear. Again her tormentor's wife tried to intervene, and this time the man not only snarled at her but struck her too, so violently that she staggered and almost fell. For a few seconds there was a tense silence, and the man seemed to gain control of himself. He took a step towards Hanae and she cringed back, retching against the gag; but he did not touch her. Instead he spoke comparatively coolly, which somehow seemed to make what he said all the more menacing.

"Listen very carefully to me," he said. "I don't intend to repeat this. *I want that netsuke.* Either you know where it is or your husband does. Now you are going to record a short message to him on tape. You are going to tell him

141

that if the netsuke is not in my possession very soon I shall describe to him in detail your naked body and what I intend to do to it. If the netsuke is in your house you are to tell me exactly where it is, and to warn your husband to call off any police surveillance whatsoever during the time it takes me to arrange for it to be collected. If you have been telling the truth and really do not know where it is, then you are to make your husband understand that he must have it delivered to a place I will tell you. Don't allow yourself to entertain any doubt that I mean what I say. Understand clearly that if I do not get what I want by the time I specify, you will suffer. In ways that neither you nor he will wish to contemplate.''

The menacing voice went on, the horror of what he was saying magnified by the distinctly pompous, public-speaking manner in which he expressed himself. Hanae was sick with dread, and her whole body crawled with animal terror as he went on.

Eventually he fell silent, and it was the other woman who now spoke. ''He would do it, believe me,'' she said very quietly, and it was this which persuaded Hanae that she could resist no longer. The man seemed to sense that he had broken her spirit at last, and asked in a matter-of-fact way whether she was now ready to cooperate. Hanae nodded miserably, and he untied the gag almost casually as she desperately tried to prevent her breasts from brushing against his clothing.

He still made no attempt to touch her body, but she saw the hood move as he looked her up and down for a long moment, then crossed quickly to a cupboard in a corner of the room and took from it a batter-powered cassette recorder. ''Do you know where the netsuke is?'' he demanded, and Hanae nodded again, swallowing drily and licking her sore lips.

He took a small notebook from his pocket, and a ballpoint pen. ''Very well. I want to know exactly where it is, and I shall then write down what you are to say.'' He switched on a table lamp and sat ready to write. "No," he snapped at the woman who must be his wife. "Don't untie her arms. She must be aware of the consequences if the results are not what is required." The woman shrank away from Hanae, who nevertheless looked at her with forlorn gratitude. The man asked the question formally, as though eliciting a statement of evidence in court. "What is the precise location of the netsuke?"

Bruised in body and sick with terror at the possible implications, Hanae told him a convincing string of lies.

Chapter XVII

OTANI WAS VERY FAR FROM A STATE OF MIND IN WHICH he could think clearly, and had no thought of apologising to Noguchi, who lumbered rapidly but awkwardly down the stairs behind him and Kimura, his head swaying from side to side as though he were a wounded bull. His suspicion of Noguchi had mounted so steadily, and such a monstrous conviction had grown in his mind, that the brief violence of the drama in his office had done little more than defuse his murderous rage, leaving him weak and drained. His thoughts were disordered and undirected, but a small cold residue of common sense prevented him from trying to challenge the leadership Kimura had imposed on both him and Noguchi.

Migishima was waiting in the entrance hall, and a patrol car was drawn up outside, the red lamp on its roof already flashing. It was not Otani's car and the driver was not Tomita; and these entirely understandable departures from his normal pattern of behaviour reinforced Otani's sensation of being swept along in the hands of others. Part of him hated it, but he suffered himself to be bundled into the back of the car and unprotestingly made room for Kimura and for Noguchi's bulk, as Migishima flung himself in the front beside the driver.

It was before nine in the evening, and the entertainment quarter of Kobe was full of activity. As Noguchi and Kimura conferred quietly together, with Migishima leaning back from the front, all eager attention, Otani felt oddly detached. At one point he heard Kimura brusquely order the driver not to use the siren, but even so the flashing red light had its effect and taxis and private cars pulled over to make way for the black and white Toyota Police Special.

A strange, dreamy calm came over Otani as the car took a corner into the main road near the Ikuta Shrine and he noticed that there seemed to be some kind of local festival going on. The sound of gongs rose up above the commonplace bustle of traffic noise, and the driver swerved to avoid a straggling procession of children in short cotton happi-coats with the name of the shrine printed on the binding in bold Chinese characters. Behind them came ten or a dozen boisterous young men in the same kind of purple, black and white short jacket over tight white shorts. They were carrying an ornately carved and gilded portable wooden shrine about the size of a tea-chest, mounted on two long shafts. Although its weight was well within their capacity to handle, they swayed and whooped, ostentatiously pretending to drop their burden from time to time and careering from side to side as though about to bump into the small but admiring crowd of spectators, whose mood seemed as merry as their own. In his boyhood Otani had occasionally taken part in very similar processions, the bearers boastfully demonstrating their lack of awe in being entrusted with parading the local tutelary Shinto deity round the district; though by the time he had reached the age of the young men actually carrying the portable tabernacle there had

145

been little sense of revelry in a Japan rapidly coming to face the inevitability of defeat in war.

The contrast between the medieval atmosphere of the procession and the smart shops and restaurants nearby, most of them still open for business and with plenty of customers, was not particularly striking to Japanese, and none of the other men in the car gave the spectacle more than a casual glance. As they drove on alongside the arches of the national railway line which runs east and west and bisects the city of Kobe, the elegance of the smartest part of the city was soon supplanted by the gaudiness of cheap restaurants, *pachinko* pin-ball parlours and noisy bars with crudely painted signs outside depicting improbably endowed hostesses in filmy gauze nightdresses. For three thousand yen one could enjoy the relatively undivided attention of one of them while drinking a small bottle of beer and eating a handful of peanuts: a sultan for half an hour. Further along were the Turkish baths and "pink" cinemas. The car was held up as they passed one, and Otani shuddered as his gaze focused on the display of posters and photographs outside. The film being shown and the coming attractions seemed all to be concerned with sexual sadism, and he heard again the thick sensual voice on the telephone as he wrenched his eyes away from a picture of a naked girl trussed up with ropes looking in terror at a middle aged man in horn-rimmed glasses reaching out a coarse hand towards one erect nipple.

A sour, bitter bile rose up in this throat, and as the car moved forward again he turned and looked at Kimura, who sensed his movement and spoke to him directly for the first time since they had left headquarters. "Don't worry, Chief," he said, using his habitual colloquial form of address again after what seemed a very long time. Otani was oddly comforted, sensing obscurely that he had been readmitted to decent society. "We're being very careful not to raise the alarm. One of Ninja's plain-clothes men is already keeping an eye on the place and we'll leave the car in a

146

minute. It's very fortunate. There's a *sake* bar right next door, and the owner owes Ninja a favour.''

The phrase rang very familiarly to Otani; he had heard it so often before. Kobe seemed to be full of seedy entrepreneurs, pursuing a variety of occupations, who owned Noguchi favours. Otani said nothing, but nodded and met Kimura's eyes. Kimura seemed to be reassured by what he saw, and nobody spoke for the remaining few minutes as the driver negotiated some increasingly ill-lit streets and finally pulled up quietly beside a bulldozer perched on a mound of earth on a small site between a dingy old-fashioned rice shop and a tiny open-fronted establishment where they made the festive roundels of brightly coloured paper flowers and fabric streamers used to mark the opening of new restaurants of the cheaper kind, and which tended to remain outside such establishments until their increasingly grubby tattiness prompted their removal.

As everyone except the driver got out of the car a figure emerged from the shadows behind the bulldozer and approached Noguchi. He was a thin, sharp-faced man in the breeches and rubber-soled work shoes with a separate compartment for the big toe often worn by manual labourers, especially in the construction trade. After a whispered conference with Noguchi he made off past the rice shop, which seemed to be open for business in a half-hearted sort of way. It was illuminated by a single low-wattage electric bulb dangling unshaded from its wire, and the old man who sat poring over a lurid comic surrounded by sacks of rice and a few four-kilo plastic bags ready for sale looked up without much curiosity as the four others followed their guide; then resumed his reading.

They were still not very far from the railway, but on the other side of the tracks, and in an area which Otani recognised as one of the poorest districts in the city. Although there were one or two seedy inns nearby which catered for the cheapest whores and their clients, they were a far cry from the Babylonian pretensions of the Fantasia Hotel with

147

its video recorders and electric beds. There was too little money in the flophouses, cheap stand-bars and eating houses for them to be of interest to the gangs, and several respectable streets of simple wooden houses and shops survived.

Noguchi's contact man led them into just such a row of two-storey wooden buildings, in the middle of which was a single more solid-looking structure of reinforced concrete with metal and glass doors on the ground floor, now dark and shuttered. This was a shop, which had a sign above the display window bearing the words "NANIWA BUTTONS". It indicated also that the business supplied fancy accessories and haberdashery to the garment trade. The upper part seemed to consist of living quarters, with separate access by way of a side door. A chink of light showed at an upstairs window. Apart from the *sake* bar next door of which Kimura had spoken, there were only one or two little shops in the dimly-lit street, among which only a general store some doors along seemed to be open, presided over by an old woman surrounded by a haphazard display of enormous packets of detergent, buckets and brooms and bright blue hosepipe on a cardboard reel. She peered at the men with beady black eyes as they passed, and muttered incomprehensibly to herself.

Noguchi pointed in silence to a narrow alleyway on the opposite side, and they all gathered in the shadows, at a point from which they could see the concrete building without much chance of being seen, though Migishima had his work cut out to disembarrass them of a small boy in striped shirt and a blue cap several sizes too big for him with the inscription *Apollo Space Mission* embroidered in English on the front, who watched them solemnly from the street.

During the waiting period Noguchi had eyed Otani warily several times, but Otani was still quiet. For Migishima it was the silence of the efficient, watchful commander of whom he stood in awe, but in their different ways Kimura and Noguchi realised that he was moving like a man in a dream, and standing quietly wherever he was put as though in a kind of catatonic trance.

Otani certainly felt light-headed and oddly detached from his body. He looked across at the darkened building no more than thirty metres away and experienced the strange conviction that he could if he wished float into the flat and float out again with Hanae in his arms. Then he rubbed his eyes and shook himself as he tried to concentrate on what Noguchi was saying in an undertone.

He caught only the tail end of the explanation, to the effect that he and Migishima would go over to the *sake* bar and make their way to the back of the haberdashery shop. The telephone from which the call had been made to Otani was in the actual shop: one of the pink payphones often put in by shopkeepers, especially in areas where there were few domestic phones. They were often operated at quite a useful profit, Noguchi added unnecessarily. Kimura and Otani were to cover the front of the premises, supported by the man in the day-labourer's clothes. Otani wondered fleetingly whether he was a police officer, but he made no attempt to identity himself and merely nodded in an off-hand way at the two senior officers he was to accompany.

Then Noguchi and Migishima were off, and the other three watched them cross the empty street. As always, Noguchi suited the seedy environment perfectly, his shabby bulk mooching into the bar as though he were one of its most regular customers. The tall, burly figure of Migishima at his side was so manifestly that of a plain-clothes police officer that the total effect was somewhat as though he had arrested the older man on suspicion, though, and Kimura made a mental note to speak to him yet again.

During the fifteen or twenty minutes which followed, Otani looked at his watch unseeingly at least a dozen times. His physical lassitude left him, to be replaced by uncontrollable fidgeting. Once, he shuddered violently and his

149

teeth chattered audibly. Kimura's lean fingers closed round his upper arm, providing an obscure and unexpected comfort. "Not long now, Chief," he said, and Otani nodded, willing him to be right. The confusion in his mind was still very great, but increasingly often the gears seemed to mesh for a while, and the frightening sense of being out of control of himself slowly faded. He swallowed, and spoke for the first time since leaving headquarters. "Should we go over to the side door?" he asked politely.

Kimura shook his head, still very much in charge. "No need. We can take anyone quite easily from here." He nodded and glanced sideways, and following the direction of his eyes, Otani saw the dull glint of the pistol in the thin man's hand. "I don't want any shooting, Kimura," he almost stammered in his alarm, just as Kimura flung himself out of the alley with Noguchi's man on his heels.

By the time Otani gathered his wits and ran across to help them the brief struggle was almost over, and Kimura had his man in a judo stranglehold. Noguchi's undercover man was limping and cursing in an undertone as he rubbed at his right leg, and it was Otani who responded to Kimura's grunt order to get the handcuffs from his right-hand jacket pocket. It had been a long time since Otani had personally handcuffed a man, and a fierce triumph rose up in him as Kimura skillfully forced his captive to his knees and Otani snapped the cuffs on behind his back. The wrists were thick and they would chafe. Otani noted the fact dispassionately. The he noticed something else. The man grunting and panting on his knees was wearing a dark pin-striped suit which even in the ill-lit street was obviously of the highest quality, and in the lapel of the jacket was a badge. This was not in itself remarkable. When in civilian clothes Otani himself customarily displayed with pride his Rotary badge. His fellow Rotarians of the Kobe South Club would have been shocked were he to appear at a regular Tuesday lunchtime meeting without it. Employees of prestigious Japanese companies invariably wear lapel badges, and the symbols of Mitsubishi, Sumitomo, Mitsui and the others are seen on every commuter train. Painful decisions sometimes need to be made when a company executive achieves such seniority as to be admitted to the exclusive ranks of Rotary, and Otani had occasionally noticed such men surreptitiously changing badges as they arrived at the New Port Hotel for the club meeting.

The emblem in this man's lapel was even more special. It was quite large and consisted of a golden chrysanthemum raised up on an opulent indigo velvet mount with a short silken cord curling away behind the lapel. Badges like it were to be seen every day on the television news, but only rarely on the streets, since their owners generally travelled in comfortably appointed cars. It was the badge of a member of the House of Councillors of the National Diet of Japan, and the man Otani and Kimura had arrested could only be Yoshihisa Yago.

The side door to the flat above the haberdashery shop was still open, and Migishima emerged, propelling before him with evident unease a woman, who took one look at the handcuffed man on his knees in the street and collapsed in Migishima's arms. By now the little boy in the Apollo Space Mission cap had returned, and two men with faces flushed from *sake* were half in and half out of the bar, gazing with fascination at the drama in the street. Kimura gave a series of crisp instructions, and Migishima, with Noguchi's anonymous assistant, pulled the Dietman to his feet and marched him off towards the patrol car, leaving Kimura in temporary charge of the woman. "Two more cars!" he barked after Migishima. "One for us, and one for the Superintendent and Mrs Otani."

As he spoke a light was switched on inside the side entrance, revealing a flight of stairs. Unusually for Japan, they were carpeted. A moment later, Noguchi came down, alone. He approached Otani, a strange expression on his

151

face, and Otani always swore to Hanae afterwards that his heart actually stopped beating until an awkward smile spread over his old colleague's leathery features.

"She's all right," he muttered. "You'd better go up."

Chapter XVIII

"**I**'M REALLY NOT ILL, YOU KNÓW," HANAE INSISTED gently, propped up as she was rather awkwardly in the downstairs living-room in their house at Rokko. It had been distinctly embarrassing when Inspector Noguchi of all people had burst into the living room seconds after the sound of the crashing of glass from the bedroom, closely followed by Migishima, who had taken one look at Hanae, gone brick-red and set off in pursuit of the man in the hood, who was out of the door immediately, pulling the hood off as he went. Noguchi called Migishima back at once, and leaving him to deal with the woman, gently untied Hanae's wrists and himself pulling the kimono up over her shoulders and covered her body almost before she realised what was happening. Then elation took hold of her, and she began to babble her gratitude, only to become bewildered when Noguchi turned away and supervised the removal of the woman, first jerking the hood off her head.

The face of the collector for the Society of Helping Handicapped Koreans was a mask of exhaustion and despair, and Hanae felt a flicker of sympathy for her as their eyes met and Migishima pulled her towards the door, as limp and lifeless as a rag doll beside his beefy youth. Even after that Noguchi still seemed to ignore Hanae, and several minutes seemed to elapse as he moved quickly round the flat after switching on more lights. He opened drawers and cupboards, making a rapid but fairly thorough search; then without another word made off. Hanae heard his heavy footfalls going down the stairs, then a lighter, gloriously familiar tread which merged into a confusion of uncompleted words and sentences and a final hot flood of tears as Otani's arms went about her and she clung to him like a child.

Now Otani's tender incompetence was making her smile as the relief of being back in her own home flooded through her consciousness. It was not even all that late; only just after eleven, and Hanae felt warm and relaxed in a crisp clean yukata after ∩ proper bath and a simple meal of buckwheat noodles in chicken broth which Otani had insisted on preparing himself over her protests. Hanae could barely imagine what the state of the kitchen must be after his efforts. The *soba* noodles were overcooked and mushy and the broth tasted peculiar. He had put some leeks in, but had cut them up so clumsily that it was difficult to manage them with chopsticks.

Otani himself was beginning to feel human again at last. The drive home in the car with Hanae huddled in his arms had been a time of utter exhaustion, even though a flicker of intellect kept telling him that the arrest of a Dietman was a very serious matter which would demand all his professional skills. It could not be left to Kimura even in his new-found masterful efficiency. Over the years Kimura had perpetrated far too many blunders and gaffes to be trusted to sort out this particular puzzle. As for Noguchi . . . Otani had to face up to the fact that he had been terribly wrong in his interpretation of this part in the jigsaw, but it would still need to be illuminated thoroughly before Otani could trust him as completely as in the past.

154

It really did seem that Hanae had suffered no real harm. No physical harm, at least. Otani bathed her himself when they arrived back at the house in Rokko, sponging her body so gently that Hanae almost drifted off to sleep during his ministrations. Her wrists were bruised, and there was an angry weal across her cheek, but apart from these and the dark puffiness under her eyes she bore no marks of bodily ill-treatment.

There were a thousand things he burned to ask her about her ordeal, but all Otani's professionalism deserted him as he sat on the tatami matting near her, nodding with exhaustion himself as the waves of relief continued to sweep through him. It would have been difficult to guess even roughly how many hundreds of hours of interrogation Otani had undertaken during the course of his police career, and he had often continued probing the mind of a witness or a suspect almost oblivious to the passage of time and to his own need for food and rest. He was good at it. Even among a people whose whole language and psychological conditioning tended them towards allusiveness, hints and evasions, Otani's delicate skill in drifting round a subject, illuminating it now from one, now from another aspect, was remarkable.

Nevertheless, confronted with the prospect of asking his own wife what had happened to her in the past forty-eight hours Otani shrank back, and became clumsy and diffident. The fact that Hanae's experiences were materially relevant to a complex criminal investigation with political implications made for even worse confusion in his tired mind. He had recovered enough of his balance to be aware that he had been dangerously out of control himself and had been saved by the professionalism and loyalty of Kimura: he wished he could feel the same about Noguchi.

Eventually, after smiling stupidly at Hanae for a long moment as she wriggled into a more comfortable position, Otani replied. "Perhaps not. But you've had a terrible ex-

155

perience. Tomorrow, when you're rested, I shall have to ask you to tell me everything that happened.''

Hanae nodded quietly. ''Was it really only the day before yesterday that you went to Tokyo? I've lost all track of time.''

Otani looked at his wrist watch. ''Yes. It's just after eleven now. Just about this time I was ringing and ringing from Tokyo and getting into a real panic when there was no reply.''

''Did you think I'd run off with the fishmonger?'' Hanae smiled with a hint of wickedness as she came out with the stock Japanese joke, and suddenly remembered how surprised she had been to be told by one of her well-travelled friends at the YWCA cookery class that in England it seemed that milkmen had the same sort of reputation there. It was hard enough to imagine such a profession, let alone to credit that its members enjoyed vivid sex lives.

Otani felt himself colour slightly, and hoped Hanae wouldn't notice. ''No, not the fishmonger,'' he said truthfully.

Hanae lay back and closed her eyes. ''Of course not. You could have hardly thought it would be a politician who wanted me in his wicked clutches.'' Even as she spoke, Hanae wondered what imp of perversity had possessed her that she should be teasing her beloved and exhausted husband even gently. Perhaps it was the fact that the past days had entailed such an extraordinary dislocation of her normally agreeable but uneventful routine that made her want to make Otani aware of her as a person in her own right, rather than a part of ''inside the house'', as Japanese wives are referred to by their own husbands. She admitted to herself that she had greatly enjoyed her conversation over coffee with Kimura and been more stimulated than she would ever have imagined by the touch of his hand on her arm. Then again, even in her terror and revulsion there had been a tiny element of excitement as she had been forced

156

to submit half-naked to the rough handling of the man in the flat.

Otani sat bolt upright. "Did he . . . ? I mean, were you . . . ?" He was floundering and when she opened her eyes again Hanae saw that his face was red.

She relented, at least a little. "With his wife in the room? Hardly . . ."

Otani was left uneasily aware that his implied question had been answered, but that Hanae had not actually reassured him about the Dietman's possible intentions or indeed her likely response if the situation had been different, and blundered on inexcusably. "You mean that if his wife hadn't been there you might have . . . you aren't telling me you already knew him, are you?"

Momentarily Hanae's expression stiffened, then she smiled rather coolly. "Well, after all, I wasn't wearing very much, was I? I got the impression that he didn't find me actually hideous . . . and whatever you may think about him, he's certainly a masterful sort of man . . ."

Stunned, Otani stared at her in horror, his mood of drowsy relaxation utterly dispelled. For the very first time since he had first known her, he was seized with a terrible desire to strike her.

Hanae sensed that she had gone too far, and threw off the quilt which Otani had arranged round her shoulders. Then she flung herself at him and hugged him furiously. "Oh, you *stupid* man! Can't you see I was just teasing you? He was horrible, I've never seen him before in my life and I was frightened out of my wits . . ."

Otani cradled her and they both babbled apologies until the crisis was past.

Then he held her at arms length and looked at her soberly. "I nearly hit you," he admitted.

"I know. Really we're behaving like a pair of romantic teenagers instead of a solemn old middle-aged couple. Still, respectable grandmothers don't get kidnapped every day. You must try to forgive me for making the most of it."

Hanae seemed to have thrown off her tiredness, and there was a sparkle in her eyes. "Do you know," she demanded, "you haven't even asked about the netsuke? That shows you *must* care more about me than you do about your work."

The pleasure in her face reassured Otani even as he wrenched his mind back to the whole muddy confusion of the investigation that Hanae at least seemed not to be worried about the whereabouts of the quaint little carving at its centre. He nodded. "I thought I was much too tired to even care about the wretched thing. All right. Where is it?"

Hanae was aware, even in her new mood of gaiety, that the time for teasing had passed. "I'll fetch it," she said, and disappeared into the kitchen, coming back a moment later with a jar of dark imported marmalade cold from the refrigerator, a fork and a small plate. "I might have known," he said wrily as he took the lid off, then probed gently with the fork. The jar was two-thirds full, and the marmalade completely concealed the netsuke in the shroud of plastic wrap with which Hanae had protected it. Fishing it out, Otani teased the plastic covering open with the fork and two fingers, which he licked absent-mindedly as he contemplated the little Clio, unmarked, surrounded by smears of English marmalade.

"Whatever happened to me, you would surely have found it eventually," said Hanae proudly, and Otani heaved a huge sigh.

"Well done," he said, using the conventional phrase, but with a sincerity that came through. "Well, there's a patrolman on duty outside, but I think we'll take the lady to bed with us to be on the safe side. Shall I carry you upstairs?"

Hanae shook her head. "I don't want you to have a heart attack tonight of all nights," she said, and smiled again a little ambiguously. "I feel quite wide awake, actually . . ."

Chapter XIX

KIMURA AND NOGUCHI MADE THEIR WAY ON FOOT through the narrow alleys from the haberdashery shop towards the main road. The weather was still splendid, and the translucent blue sky high above transformed the look of the mean and cluttered back streets through which they passed. Kimura sniffed the air appreciatively. "Can you smell curry?" he enquired. "I'm hungry."

Noguchi's face was its habitual leathery mask, but he rumbled his agreement and led the way to a shabby little eating house. Its sliding door was open and they pushed through the dark blue divided cotton curtain hanging in the entrance. The interior was surprisingly clean, containing only three plastic topped tables each with a beaker full of pairs of new wooden chopsticks in their paper wrappers, a smaller container of toothpicks and a soy-sauce dispenser. The inevitable television set fizzed and crackled on its shelf high in one corner, and hand-written paper streamers implied that the menu was limited to curry with rice or mixed fried rice in the Chinese manner. It was eleven fifteen and early for lunch even in Japan, so they had the place to themselves. Having served their generous helpings of enigmatic curry over great mounts of white rice and a bottle of beer apiece, the motherly proprietress disappeared from view as the two men unwrapped the tin spoons from the flimsy paper napkins which had been placed before them and attacked their lunch.

"Strange sort of place for a wealthy woman to rent a flat," Kimura mused as he filled Noguchi's beer glass and then his own.

Noguchi took a deep draught and belched with satisfaction. "Owner's in the clear. No connection with Yago that I can find. Advertised the flat . . . ordinary way, estate agent. High rent for the neighbourhood. Woman comes along, quiet word, down payment in cash, needs a flat to meet her lover now and then. Very handy, I believe him."

Kimura nodded in agreement. "Yes, it rang true. Anyway, you say your people round here confirm that's what she used to do. What is it, over a year now it would be?"

"Couple of times a week on average. Stupid when you come to think of it. Much cheaper to go to a short-time hotel." Noguchi's movements were ponderous, but he was disposing of his curry with extraordinary speed, and had cleared his plate long before Kimura dealt with half of his. Even so, he sat back quietly with his beer as Kimura theorised at some length between mouthfuls.

"My feeling is that her husband found out somehow about her affair just about the time the Old Man let it out that he had the netsuke. Had too much on his mind to do more than register the fact. Just what he needed to blackmail his wife into helping him snatch Mrs Otani and a convenient place to take her. If he murdered the Filipino woman he'd be ready to take a good many chances."

"He did." Noguchi said.

"Did what?"

"Murder Ventura."

Kimura put down his spoon and pushed his plate away. "Well, I wish I were as sure as you. Young Migishima has been picking away quite well at Yago's business connections. He certainly has money in the Love Box Cabaret where the foreign girls work, but the tie-up with the hotel is more complicated . . .''

He broke off as he realised that Noguchi had begun to shake his big head slowly from side to side. "Police Training Manual stuff. Migishima's a good boy, but he should have come to me." Noguchi looked round as another customer walked in and as if by magic the proprietress reappeared and shouted a cheery welcome. "Come on," he said, and hauled himself to his feet, pulling a crumpled thousand-yen note from his pocket and handing it to Kimura.

Outside in the street Kimura explained in some detail that the total bill had amounted only to fourteen hundred and fifty, but Noguchi waved away the proferred two hundred and seventy-five from his half share and made off, with Kimura in his wake. "Yago gets money from a medium-size gang affiliated to the Yamamoto network," he was saying as Kimura fell into step beside him again. "It's called the General Help Club, and it owns the Fantasia Hotel and two or three more in town. Yago generally used the Fantasia, and was never given a bill."

"So you say," Kimura's response was wary. He knew too much of Noguchi's methods and network of informants to challenge so definite a statement outright. Besides, Migishima had already traced a similar connection without Noguchi's help.

Noguchi came to an abrupt halt and looked squarely at Kimura. "So I *know*. Haven't been wasting my time, Kimura. No question he killed that tart. Hard to prove it. None of the hotel people going to identify him if they can help it."

"All right. I suppose you've been working on that character Nakayama. The one who takes care of the *gaijin* talent. Don't forget the situation with the Old Man, though."

They walked on. "You handled him quite well," Noguchi conceded gruffly.

It was praise indeed coming from him, and even though Kimura was quite well aware that he deserved it, he was gratified. "Thank you, Ninja," he said graciously. "All the same, he's still very peculiar about you. It seems to me that he won't lay everything out until he knows where you stand. I wouldn't mind knowing myself, as a matter of fact."

"Better, is he?" Noguchi's manner was as perfunctory as if he were enquiring about somebody with a cold in the head. "Didn't see him yesterday." They had reached the main road and waited obediently with a little knot of other pedestrians until the light had turned to green.

"Much better. He rang me first thing to say he'd be into headquarters late, and turned up about half past ten looking almost back to normal. Had a long talk on the phone with the district prosecutor, then sent for me and talked quite sensibly about the whole business. It seems his wife didn't come to any real harm."

Noguchi grunted. "Say anything about the netsuke?"

Kimura grinned reminiscently. "He did more. Showed the blessed thing to me at last and made me watch him put it in his safe. Funny little thing. That was after we got the photographer up with a magnifying lens and photographed the scratch marks on it. Results not as good as the ones the museum camera produced from the others, but legible. Then we went down and had a first go at Yago and his wife. Later he told me to rope you in to sort out this business with the owner of the flat this morning, while he was with the prosecutor. I had a job talking him into calling you to this afternoon's session, I can tell you. He's still not at all sure whose side you're on."

"Soon find out, won't he?" They were nearing police headquarters and the streets were full of office workers at the height of the lunch break. "One thirty, was it?"

Kimura looked at his watch. It had stopped again. The

confounded thing seemed to eat batteries and he resolved there and then to acquire one of the new Seiko hybrid versions with actual hands. It might well prove to be a great convenience. "Yes," he said. "It's about half past twelve now. We'd better go up together. We don't want him going for you again." Noguchi actually smiled, and they agreed to meet in the main entrance five minutes ahead of time. Then Noguchi disappeared in the direction of the scruffy office he so rarely used, and Kimura decided to fortify himself with a coffee. There was a pleasant quiet place just beside the bank, and he had time to get some cash from the dispensing machine as well before making his way back to the shabby old headquarters building where Noguchi was already waiting for him. Unbelievably, he was wearing a necktie.

They mounted the broad stairs in silence and walked along the corridor towards Otani's room. Kimura glanced at Noguchi, who was staring woodenly ahead. Although never a forthcoming man, his silence on this occasion amounted to a positive emanation, and Kimura was apprehensive as he tapped on Otani's door and they heard his brisk invitation to enter. It was almost exactly one-thirty.

Otani was in uniform, and was standing rigidly to attention beside the filing cabinet beyond the low table and precisely squared-off easy-chairs used for informal meetings, his back to the gloomy painting on the wall. Noguchi shouldered past Kimura and marched towards Otani, stood facing him and bowed formally. It was a courtesy Kimura had never before seen him offer, and the effect was so stunning that he remained near the door watching.

"I have offended, and I ask your pardon." Noguchi's tones were clipped and correct, his habitual manner of speech absent. Kimura could have sworn he saw Otani blink hard as he bowed low in response and replied with equally formal apologies for his own actions. Then the two older men stood in silence as Otani's eyes searched Noguchi's face, reading its apparently impassive expression with the

163

subtlety derived from long years of friendship. At last the tension relaxed, and Otani turned half away with an odd, weary little gesture as Kimura stepped forward towards his usual easy-chair.

"It's time for plain speaking," Otani said in a normal conversational voice. "You do see that, don't you, both of you?" He gestured towards the chairs and sank heavily into his own.

Noguchi was the last to sit and he waited till he was settled before replying. "Yes. Should have spoken out sooner. Might have avoided all this. All right, is she?" His resumption of taciturn offhandedness was not wholly convincing, and it was as though he was reaching out with a tendril of warmth in search of an answering gesture from Otani.

At last Otani's eyes softened, and he smiled very briefly. "She'll be all right. Thanks to you both. Still rather shaken, naturally. So am I, for that matter. I'll be pleased if we can keep a man on duty outside the house for a day or two more." He sat in silence for a few seconds, then looked from Kimura to Noguchi with a new alertness. "Well, let's get started. Right from the beginning. I haven't been entirely straight with you two, so I'll kick off. You know I don't like to interfere in your cases, Kimura-kun, but some time ago I took it into my head to pay a visit to the Fantasia Hotel to have a look around. I didn't want them to know who I was, so I took my wife along . . ."

The atmosphere changed remarkably as Otani's monologue proceeded, and by the time he finally ended his account all three men had fallen into the attitudes most natural to them during their conferences. Kimura was sitting daintily working with one fingernail on the cuticles of the others, legs crossed carefully to avoid creasing his trousers; while Noguchi seemed to have fallen into a deep slumber, his eyes closed. Otani himself had recovered his slightly schoolmasterly eloquence, and to some extent the pleasure in the sound of his own voice which was the characteristic he would have been most horrified to have pointed out to him.

When Otani broke off he demanded green tea, and Kimura buzzed for some to be fetched. They all sipped the aromatic brew Otani preferred, even Noguchi. "Your turn, Ninja. It had better be good." His use of Noguchi's nickname for the first time since Hanae's abduction was encouraging, but there was still a wariness about him, and a slight chill descended as Noguchi began his own statement.

Extended narrative was not his strong point, and Noguchi's contribution came in fits and starts. Once or twice Kimura opened his mouth to interject a comment, but on each occasion intercepted a warning glare from Otani and reluctantly subsided again.

Though disjointed, it was an interesting story. Noguchi confirmed that as a member of the provost detachment at staff headquarters of the Imperial Japanese Army of occupation in the Philippines he had worked in close proximity to General Yago, the father of the Dietman now in the cells below. Needless to say there was a good deal of speculation about the personality and interests of the General, whose passion for the fine arts was well publicised. His staff had found a number of valuable pieces for him, but the more interesting rumour was that he had amassed a huge quantity of gold as a result of a series of seizures from bank vaults and smaller quantities confiscated from private owners. This had ostensibly been shipped to Japan, but a persistent rumour had it that the general had personally arranged for it to be buried in a remote spot well away from Manila itself.

Almost as an afterthought Noguchi mentioned that like most of the other senior officers the general had taken a Filipino mistress rather than patronising the Japanese prostitutes sent to Manila for their pleasure, and that he had been known to be greatly attached to her, especially after she bore him a baby daughter. "Cleo. Odd sort of name.

165

Never knew what he called the kid, but struck me a while ago that the Ventura woman was about the right age . . ."

Noguchi's rumbling voice trailed off, and Kimura emitted a strangled squawk of outrage before being silenced by an impatient gesture from Otani. "I've said it before and I'll say it again. Either we three trust each other or we don't. I accept that you thought you were acting in my interests, Ninja. Nevertheless, this whole business needn't have got out of hand if you had told us all this at the outset." He coloured slightly. "As I said earlier, I blame myself too. In fact you're the only one who seems to have gone by the book, Kimura."

Mollified by the compliment, Kimura extended both hands in an expansive gesture of forgiving and forgetting. "Well, we seem to be on course at last, and high time too. At least our idea about the map reference seems to have been a good one. We've got eight of the nine fragments now. I wonder if the experts can pinpoint the place without the last one? Presumably the general gave the netsuke to the girl's mother but the girl never realised the significance. The question is, what did he do with the last one?"

Otani was enthused. It was quite like old times again. "Look, it all fits in," he said eagerly. "Don't you see, it accounts for the extraordinary lengths Yago went to as soon as he discovered that I'd got hold of the eighth one. He must have the ninth, and he must know well enough that the full map reference can only be read from the whole set. The general must have managed to give him the last one before he was arrested and tried as a war criminal. We can easily check whether Yago tried to trace his half-sister . . . extraordinary business. Certainly motive enough for murdering her once he found her if she refused to help him . . . but on the other hand it would rule out any chance of his ever getting hold of the remaining netsuke." He sat back and tried pushing his lips in and out in the manner of Nero Wolfe, but still failed to see a way out of the puzzle,

166

even though Wolfe was almost his favourite fictional detective.

"The picture's a lot clearer than it was, but there's a long way to go yet," he concluded eventually.

"How did you get on with the prosecutor?" Kimura asked rather sharply. He was irritated at having had to surrender the initiative he had been exercising with some satisfaction even while greatly worried over Otani's near-breakdown of the preceding days; and his question was intended as a veiled warning to Otani not to keep things to himself again.

"Yes, the prosecutor." Otani sighed. "Well, you might expect, the mere fact of our arresting a member of the Diet has set the wires humming between here and Tokyo. Never mind that we caught him red-handed as a kidnapper and that he's almost certainly committed murder. He has a lot of powerful friends in the political establishment, not to mention plenty of people to cover up for him among the *yakuza* here . . . All the same, we're not going to let him wriggle out of this . . ." He fell silent as the sense of outrage still fresh in him boiled up, and fumbled in his tunic pocket for a cigarette which Kimura leaned forward to light for him.

"Yago's a tough character," Kimura conceded. "You had him bothered by the end of our session with him yesterday, though. And we didn't even know all this stuff Ninja's given us."

Noguchi opened an eye, and growled. "No bail for this one. Let me lean on him a bit."

Otani stubbed out the cigarette barely started, and looked at his watch. "It's going to need careful handling by all of us," he said. "And from now on we'll keep each other fully in the picture. Understood?"

It was evident to Kimura and Noguchi that he was feeling a great deal better.

Chapter XX

"**I** DON'T FEEL IN THE LEAST LIKE GOING TO A WEDding," Otani grumbled as Hanae adjusted his grey and white striped tie for him. "You look very nice, though," he admitted, looking her up and down in a way that made her cheeks go pink. Hanae was as a matter of fact looking splendid, in her formal black kimono with a splash of silver decoration near the hem and the crest of the Otani family on each sleeve near the shoulder and high on her slender back. She had been to the beauty shop earlier in the day and her hair was a miracle of glossy perfection.

The previous evening indeed Otani had begun to complain that Hanae looked altogether too excited about what would undoubtedly be an extremely tedious occasion. No doubt Migishima and Woman Patrolman Terauchi had reason to be in a twitter on the eve of their wedding, carefully timed to take place on a propitious "Maximum Peace" day according to the old Chinese reckoning. There was no need for Hanae to fuss like a startled virgin, though. He even alleged that she was making more of it than when their own daughter Akiko had been married.

He struggled mutinously into his rented tailcoat, then peered from the tiny entrance hall of their house to make sure that the taxi from the hire company was still there. They had plenty of time, but in spite of his protestations of rebellion he had no intention of allowing them to arrive late at the reception at the wedding hall in Kobe.

Hanae took a last look at herself in the small mirror in the living-room and then joined Otani, stepping down from the dark polished wooden step delicately into her new decorative sandals, already in position in the hall. She had small, neat feet, and the snow-white *tabi* socks she was wearing peeped demurely from under her rich silk kimono. Otani glanced at her curiously yet again as the driver of the hire car leapt out to hold the door open for them: old-fashioned action rendered unnecessary in ordinary taxis by the universal installation of the automatic door-opening devices operated from the driver's seat. Hanae had an odd, almost smug expression on her face as she patted her bulky obi, immaculately in position as it was round her waist. Otani would have given a good deal to know more about the mysterious errand which had kept her out of the house for most of the previous afternoon. She had telephoned him to warn him that she would be out for two or three hours.

Hanae prattled cheerfully on the way in from the suburbs of Rokko to central Kobe, dwelling mostly on the honeymoon plans of Migishima and his bride, which were common gossip all through police headquarters and concerning which Hanae had quizzed Otani remorselessly. It was very early December, and though Otani pointed out that the weather in Japan was still delightfully mild, Hanae waxed jealously effusive about the balmy sunshine of Hawaii. Although the Otanis' presence at the wedding reception was absolutely essential, they would be spared the duty of going to Osaka International Airport to see the newly-weds off, and since the actual ceremony was set for noon and the reception would be over by two-thirty at the latest, they

169

would be home by three with the rest of the day to themselves.

The Central Wedding Hall not far from the Ikuta Shrine had a financial arrangement with the Shinto authorities whereby the shrine priest normally officiated in the small chapel built into the complex of restaurants, beauty salons and photographic studios which was designed to cope with as many as twenty receptions a day at the busy season. Woman Patrolman Terauchi's parents, it turned out, must have been quite well-to-do. Instead of the all-in package for the ceremony and catering for a total of forty persons which was the most popular deal by far, they had arranged for the exchange of *sake* cups and votive offerings to take place in the Ikuta shrine itself, and as Hanae and Otani waited in the lounge of the wedding hall for the other guests to assemble it became clear that the reception must have been laid on for at least a hundred guests.

Only a dozen or so were over at the shrine to witness the actual ceremony, of course. That privilege was reserved for the immediate family, the priest and one or two shrine virgins, plus of course the go-between. The Otanis had a good half hour to wait, but were comfortable enough sipping the special ''joyful'' tea provided and nodding from time to time in acknowledgement of greetings from various police officers who approached them to pay their respects.

Kimura looked dazzling in striped trousers and morning coat which fitted him so sleekly that he looked like a model in a magazine. He bowed very low before the Otanis and Hanae found herself avoiding his eye as they chatted. Fortunately her confusion was short-lived, since very soon the master of ceremonies, who apparently was the bride's elder brother, announced that guests were requested to take their places in the reception room. He held the microphone too close to his mouth, and an eerie scream accompanied his words.

As befitted their distinguished status, the Otanis were ushered to places very close to the top table, and sat down

170

before a great armoury of knives, forks and spoons. An expectant hush fell over the room and a disturbance at the main entrance arose briefly and then subsided again as the strains of Mendelssohn's Wedding March filled the large room and the guests rose in their places at the round tables, each with its sign on a stand in the centre as an aid to *placement*. Apart from tables labelled Pine, Plum, Bamboo and Chrysanthemum, there were rather more imaginative ones like Iris, Rose and Maple. The Otanis were sharing Maple with two other couples, and had a clear view of the little procession as it wended its way among the tables under the lights of the chandeliers.

The bride and groom were preceded by the master of ceremonies. Migishima looked very fine in full classical male dress, the black silk of his short *haori* jacket with crests similar to those on Hanae's kimono contrasting with the striped blue and grey of the stiff *hakama* divided skirt which came to his ankles below. He strode with rocklike dignity: a fairly easy matter since on his feet were simple flat sandals of fine woven straw. The new Mrs Migishima had a much more difficult time of it, hobbled as she was by the tight folds of her wedding kimono and having to teeter along on elevated lacquer *geta* as well as balancing the heavy headdress of brocade on her bewigged head. At her side her mother held her elbow, occasionally helping when a fold of the stiff brocade caught on her daughter's foot. The thick white pancake makeup concealed the bride's expression, and as he watched her Otani found it quite difficult to believe that the pert, almost urchin features of Woman Patrolman Junko Terauchi lay somewhere beneath it all.

Then he caught sight of Ninja Noguchi, and closed his eyes momentarily in sheer disbelief. His face suffused with colourful embarrassment, his eyes fixed firmly on a point somewhere high on the back wall of the room, Noguchi brought up the rear, oblivious to the applause all around, which continued until all had taken their places at the top table. The formal wear hire people at the Daimaru Department Store had done their best with him. The trousers fitted tolerably well: men of his girth were not so very unusual, and he was positively lissom compared with a sumo wrestler. But then sumo wrestlers very sensibly go about their day-to-day business dressed in cotton yukatas, not tailcoats and striped cravats. It was the coat and waistcoat which were the problem. In order to accommodate Ninja's barrel chest it had been necessary to give him garments which were obviously far too long for him. The tails of his black coat reached almost to his ankles and the sleeves covered most of his hands.

At first Hanae wanted very much to giggle, but then, strangely, she felt tears prickling at her eyes in the face of Noguchi's vulnerability. Managing to catch his eye somehow, she put all the sympathetic warmth she could into her expression, and applauded furiously. Startled, Otani belatedly joined in, and the other guests followed suit. Perhaps because of this, and perhaps because it was after all the bride and groom who were the focus of attention, the look of acute misery on Ninja's battered face gradually faded. In any case, when sitting down on Migishima's right he looked quite impressive, and by the time he had to get up to go to the microphone to offer his formal congratulations and good wishes everyone had had a few, and both Kimura and Otani cheerfully joined in the good-humoured whoops and cheers which greeted his largely unintelligible speech.

Indeed, the Migishimas' wedding was no different from most formal Japanese occasions, in that once the ice was broken and the drinks began to flow, protocol soon broke down. As course followed course and people picked at the unfamiliar pâté, chicken in white sauce with rice *and* bread, fruit salad and ice cream, the male guests began to leave their places and wander round the room in search of cronies with whom to drink a toast.

Quite early on, the new Mrs Migishima was escorted from the room to reappear twenty minutes later dressed in

172

a formal white Western wedding dress, to another round of applause. She looked a lot less constrained, and now that it was possible to discern her facial expression, a certain timid return of her habitual almost cheeky manner was beginning to be visible. Hanae whispered to Otani, who was pulling a face at the taste of the domestic red wine he was doggedly drinking. "She looks really lovely, doesn't she?" Otani looked the bride up and down carefully. He was not really in a bad mood, and although he had never been able to understand what people saw in wine, something was making him join in the increasingly raucous barracking as speaker after speaker went to the microphone to deliver rambling and incoherent tributes to the bride and groom. The most comical contribution had, in his opinion, come from his driver Constable Tomita, who appeared from nowhere in a cheap new blue suit and seized the wandering attention of all the guests by singing a sentimental pop song. "It's a good party," he admitted. "I'm looking forward to getting you home, though. Never mind the bride."

At last it was over. The speeches became more and more desultory in the fifteen minutes after both bride and groom disappeared, and the proceedings broke up when the word was passed round that they were ready to leave the building to be driven to the airport. The Otanis joined all the other guests in the lobby as the Migishimas emerged from their changing rooms for the last time; she in a pale pink silk suit and neat white blouse, he looming over her in tropical cream linen. Hanae clasped her hands together and sighed gently. Hawaii. The very word breathed romance. Then they were off, in a hire car loaded with new white luggage, and a significant number of guests piled into taxis and cars to pursue them to the airport. Not until they were through the customs and in the departure lobby would the cameras cease to click and flash, and even then the JAL cabin crew on board the plane would cosset the newlyweds with conspiratorial indulgence all the way to Honolulu.

Otani bowed his farewells to a number of those remaining on the pavement, and ordinary passers-by skirted with incurious politeness the small group of men and women in their formal dress clutching their presents, each wrapped in a new purple cloth as delivered to the wedding hall by the department store gift service staff.

"I wonder what it is?" Hanae speculated as they sank back into their own hire car for the ride home. The custom of presenting souvenir gifts to the guests at a wedding was a burdensome expense; but one borne cheerfully enough.

"One of those presentation boxes of instant coffee, by the feel of it," said Otani, hefting the weight of their package. "We can give it to someone for New Year."

He had a slight headache, but nothing much. However, he closed his eyes during the drive back to Rokko. The Migishima wedding had loomed awkwardly in his consciousness during the protracted investigations and negotiations entailed in the clearing up of the Ventura affair. It was something of a relief to have the actual ceremony out of the way, even though very little had been required of him personally. Still, the almost daily necessity of calming down an increasingly panicky Noguchi and encouraging him to face up to his responsibilities as go-between had been a great help in restoring their former relationship and laying to rest Otani's last doubts about his old associate's role in the affair, which had brought him so near to break-down.

As the questioning of the Yagos continued and the various anxieties of the prosecutor about making the charges stick on such an influential politician were progressively stilled, it had become quite clear to Otani that Noguchi had throughout been concerned, however misguidedly, simply to protect Hanae and himself because of his knowledge of the Yago family's ruthlessness. His own confidence and skills returning, Otani had achieved solid results in breaking Yago down. It was now firmly established and recorded in formal statements that the Dietman had met Cleo Ventura in Manila. His assertion that he had no idea that she was his half-sister rang true if only because of his evident shock when confronted with the realisation that he had committed incest with her.

Slowly and with infinitely devious patience, Otani had established that the former General's son knew of the importance of gaining access to the full set of netsuke, and that this had led him to make repeated attempts to regain possession of the seven in the national collection. Under steady and subtle pressure, Yago admitted that he had recognised the one in Cleo Ventura's possession and had tried by various means to get hold of it, arousing her suspicions in the process. Until then it had been to her no more than a good luck charm.

The police now knew that it was Yago who had encouraged Cleo Ventura to return to Japan and had patronised her; and Otani's crowning success had been to extract a murder confession from Yago. It had been a curiously quiet climax to the questioning and Otani was pleased that both Kimura and Noguchi had been present when in a calm, almost matter-of-fact voice Yago finally agreed with an air of some relief that he had killed the woman in the Sweet Harmony Room of the Fantasia Hotel. Afterwards the three of them accepted that he was probably telling the truth when he claimed that he had acted in an access of blind anger when she taunted him to find the netsuke he wanted so much.

Even an influential politician does not personally commit murder with impunity. The hotel staff were sufficiently intimidated by the gang under whose protection they operated to cover up for Yago to a limited extent, but it was not a matter of too much difficulty for Kimura and Noguchi between them to clinch the confession by collateral evidence from the receptionist and the cleaning-woman who discovered the body.

It was the question of the whereabouts of the Dietman's own netsuke, Thalia, the muse of comedy, which exercised

175

Otani's mind most as the car neared the slopes of Mount Rokko and mounted towards their old house, the last in the road which finally petered out into the footpaths which criss-crossed the wooded heights. Hanae went ahead of him as he paid off the driver, and he looked for her in vain in the downstairs room. "I'm up here," came a muffled voice as Hanae heard him moving about, and Otani made his way up the polished wooden stairs, unbuttoning his waistcoat as he went.

Hanae smiled enigmatically as she helped him out of his rented finery and folded it neatly in the plastic carrying case for return to the department store the next day, and Otani grunted with relief as he slipped into the crisp clean yukata she handed him.

"Help me off with my obi," she commanded then, and turned her back. Otani fidgeted with the fastenings then furled the stiff heavy silk over one arm as Hanae twirled slowly round to unwrap herself. Her black kimono was held in place underneath the obi by narrower bands of crepe silk, and Hanae carefully untied the formal knot which secured them. Inside was a small bundle of silk, which she handed to Otani in triumph. "A present for you," she said with immense complacency as he unwrapped Thalia, the muse of comedy.

Otani sank slowly to the tatami mats and propped himself against the polished section of cypress trunk which marked off the edge of the *tokonoma* alcove with its simple arrangement of chrysanthemums in a shallow ceramic dish on the raised floor. His mouth opened and closed several times as he turned the netsuke over and over before raising his eyes to Hanae. Eventually he merely raised his eyebrows interrogatively, his lips set grimly.

"It was her buttons, you see," Hanae began, suddenly fearful that her elaborate conjuring trick might not be received with the delight she had envisaged. "There was the picture of them on the TV news and she was wearing the same coat as when she came here that night. The buttons . . ." she babbled on.

"Buttons," said Otani heavily.

"Yes. Very unusual. It just occurred to me quite suddenly. The flat over the button shop. I went back there . . . they keep an enormous stock. Hundreds of boxes, but each with samples stuck on the outside. The shopkeeper let me rummage through them—he didn't know who I was, of course—and when he saw I would probably be a long time he left me to it . . . I soon spotted the box I was looking for but I didn't want to seem too excited."

Hanae had become bright pink with embarrassment under Otani's withering glare. "I, er, I've never actually stolen anything before, and I was quite sure the man would notice when I found the netsuke in a scrap of rag underneath all the buttons in the box and slipped it in my bag. I bought quite a lot of buttons afterwards, actually." She hung her head. "So that he wouldn't suspect me," she tailed off weakly.

Hanae watched, timidly now, as Otani raised himself to his knees in silence, and then stood up, the netsuke still in one hand, his expression unreadable even by her. It seemed an eternity before he spoke, in a subdued, reflective manner. "So that he wouldn't suspect you," he said, nodding judiciously. "Well, we wouldn't want him to do that, would we?" He opened his hand and took the little carving delicately between his thumb and forefinger of the other, held it up and twisted it this way and that as he continued. "Let me see now. It should be quite simple. All I have to do is to square the Minister of Education, the Director General of the Agency for Cultural Affairs, the Superintendent General of the National Police Agency, the Director of the National Museum in Kyoto . . . oh, and we mustn't forget the legal section of the Defence Agency. They're interested in the spoils of war. The Finance Ministry and the Ministry of Foreign Affairs, of course. Then the Hyogo Public Safety

Commission because I shall need a couple of weeks' leave.''

Hanae blinked as Otani gave one of his rare huge smiles, then came forward as he opened his arms to her and hugged her before readjusting his face into the murderous *kabuki* scowl which never failed to make her weak with laughter. ''That's if I can avoid having to arrest you,'' he growled as Hanae began to recover. Hanae could scarcely string the words together, but eventually managed to enquire what on earth he thought he was talking about, and was still dabbing at her eyes when he replied. ''The Philippines, of course. Obviously, the only possible thing to do is to go and look for the gold ourselves.'' He winked solemnly, then beamed again and pretended to kiss the Muse of Comedy.

Something in Hanae's expression made the grin freeze on his face, then fade slowly as she spoke. ''Thank you, but I think I'd prefer London,'' she announced primly. ''We can stay with Akiko and her husband. She phoned yesterday to tell us he's been assigned to his company's London office for at least three years. They'll be leaving just after New Year. I thought we'd give them plenty of time to settle in and go next summer . . .''

''London? *London?*'' Otani's response was little more than a strangled croak. Tidying up the netsuke affair would be child's play in comparison.

ABOUT THE AUTHOR

James Melville was born in London in 1931 and educated in North London. He read philosophy at Birkbeck
College before being conscripted into the RAF, then
took up schoolteaching and adult education. Most of his
subsequent career has been spent overseas in cultural
diplomacy and educational development, and it was in
this capacity that he came to know, love, and write about
Japan and the Japanese. He has two sons and is married
to a singer-actress. He continues to write more mystery
novels starring Superintendent Otani.